KILL ME
A FORTUNE

KILL ME
A FORTUNE

ROBERT COLBY

WILDSIDE PRESS

Published by Wildside Press LLC
wildsidepress.com | bcmystery.com

CHAPTER 1

In a nasal monotone, Mrs. Hennessey read interminably one of her pale, pointless little stories. From my desk before the class, I looked out over the bored faces. I stifled a yawn behind my hand. I glanced at my watch. It was thirteen minutes until nine—at which time I would close the last of the Adult Education classes in creative writing before the long summer intermission.

The place was Room 204, Hillside High, Hollywood, California. It was night. Wednesday as usual. At that moment, listening to the last of Mrs. Hennessey's dreary tomes, no one could have convinced me that in the next five minutes something completely unpredictable would happen to change abruptly the listless complexion of the night. And the summer. And even my life.

The class contained a half-dozen pudgy housewives like Mrs. Hennessey. Then there was a potpourri of male office and odd-job workers. And oddball characters who apparently did nothing but chase from class to class in pursuit of "art." And finally the single girls who bunched together in the back of the room—except for Barbara Dawson, who sat always cool and alone. Twenty-one in all, and not three among them who showed the least promise. Some of my day students in English One at Hillside High could do better.

When Paul Ferris, who heads the Adult Education program, asked me to take the class, I hadn't expected he was offering me a group of ready-made talents. I knew from experience that ninety percent of all beginners were dreamers and escapees from the dull realities of living and hustling a buck. Yet I accepted. Because since I broke up with Alice Rumsey, and she got married and moved to Mexico City, I had been drifting in a gray cloud of gloom, looking impossibly for her replacement. And the two hours on Wednesday seemed a small island of relief in the brooding nights. I wanted other faces and other thoughts than my own. I wanted other problems. And because I kept the class informal and made myself an available crying towel after hours, I got them. My God, what problems! I never could go home feeling sorry for myself.

At Hillside I taught English and physical ed. An odd combination perhaps. But I'm a big guy, six-one at a hundred and ninety. I played football at UCLA, and I was pretty good at boxing. I have always been physically coordinated, and, even now at thirty-two, reasonably enthusiastic about participating sports. That's one side. The other, the spiritual you might call it, is thoughtful and complex, sensitive and decently emotional. It got me into teaching English and writing in my spare time, selling a book and maybe a couple of short stories in a lucky year. The rest has to do with personal things like my family in Denver, the girls I have known and slept with, the one or two I almost married, things like that, none of them pertinent to what happened on this particular night and thereafter.

But now Mrs. Hennessey was mouthing her poor carbon of a poor story in a typical slick magazine. And only one or two housewives, who wrote the same sort of thing were listening with rapture. The others were squirming their behinds or doodling or looking off into space.

At the left rear of the room, separated from the rest of the students by a fence of empty desks, sat Barbara Dawson. She was always last to enter the room. She came in quietly, found a remote corner, read with soft confidence when called on (not bad stuff, either), and was the first to vanish into the night. No one really knew where she went or what she was. And her attitude, though not really snooty or condescending, forbade questions. She registered for the course as living at a Hollywood hotel, claimed to be visiting from New York, and was "unemployed at present."

She was in her middle twenties and had about her a certain look and sound of elegance. The casual and simple smartness of her clothes suggested Fifth Avenue. Her long dark hair had the debutante brush and shine. She walked with erect grace and wore about her a soft cloak of poise. She read her brittle stories in a voice laced with finishing-school overtones, while nothing about her was affected or posed.

It was difficult to tell if her remoteness was natural or defensive. She was sealed within—secretive. But only about herself, her intimate thoughts and actions. In all matters concerning the class she was uninhibited, a sharp critic, eager to learn her mistakes, taking a quiet part in every discussion. But at nine o'clock she shut herself like a book and stole away.

She had not always come to the class alone. There was a time, in the beginning, when Barbara was accompanied by a young man about her age. Vandiver, his name was. Larry Vandiver. He was a very big boy, that one. Six-three maybe, and massive. But he was a puppy dog with a round face, a shy grin, and tail-wagging, obedient eyes. He was her mascot. You could almost see the invisible chain she held to the collar around his neck. Yet, though they came and went together and sat only a seat apart, she all but ignored him.

I could tell right away that he had no interest in writing. He sat beside her in his little fog of worship, sometimes scratching a note to her. (She never read the notes. With a perfectly bland face, she tore them into tiny fragments.) When called upon for an opinion, Vandiver's answers were terse and vague, as if my interruption of his reverie was an annoying imposition. He never fulfilled the smallest assignment or volunteered a comment.

"Tell me, Mr. Vandiver," I said one evening when I had to raise my voice to something like a shout to get his attention. "Tell me, why do you bother to come to this class at all?"

There was a silence, and he turned slowly to look at Barbara Dawson.

I nodded, said, "I see. Thank you very much, Mr. Vandiver."

Howls and giggles broke over the room. And that one time I saw Miss Barbara Dawson lose her composure. Her face colored and her mouth clamped in a line thin and angry as a new scar. Her eyes narrowed upon Vandiver and the bulk of him shrank in his chair.

That was the last time I saw Mr. Larry Vandiver. He never returned to the class. And though I was secretly relieved, it seemed the more natural thing to inquire after him. Besides, I was curious about Barbara and it gave me an excuse to speak to her privately. So one night as she began to fade towards the door even before the echo of my last word to the class had died, I called her name.

"Miss Dawson, just a minute, please!"

She turned with a startled look on her face, caught off balance for a moment, swaying, falling from her toes, returning with anxious frown to my desk.

"Yes, Mr. Elliot?" Long fingers with their pale-rose nails extended, tips bent, on a corner of my desk, supporting.

I looked around her, waiting until the last student had closed the door behind him.

"You wanted to speak to me, Mr. Elliot?"

"Sit down a moment, won't you, Miss Dawson?"

"I really can't stay."

"I see. Which is not always to understand." I was slightly irritated.

"I'm sorry, Mr. Elliot. It's just that I have certain obligations."

"Of course." I smiled. "I merely wanted to know what happened to your friend."

"My friend?"

"Mr. Vandiver."

"Oh." She shifted her weight and retreated to that cool sanctum behind her eyes. "Well, he's not really my friend. Just an acquaintance. I have no idea what happened to him. I haven't seen him in—well, not since…"

"The last time he was here?"

"Yes. That's right."

"I wondered why he dropped out so suddenly."

"Do you miss him?" She smiled.

"No, not really," I smiled back.

"Is there anything else, then?"

"No. I won't hold you. Nothing else. Except to say that I like your work. It develops a certain bite and power that the others lack altogether."

She brightened. "Thank you! That pleases me more than you know."

"Yes, well I mean it. Your writing has a kind of brittle conviction and authority. It moves with certainty and direction. That's good. The rest is work. Lots and lots of it."

"I'm willing. And thanks."

"You bet. Next week then. Good night."

"'Night."

She turned, clutching her notebook under her arm, paused in stride and swung back.

"Mr. Elliot," she said hesitantly. "Sometime…sometime I'd like to talk with you."

"Any time. About your writing?"

Again she hesitated. "Yes, about my writing," she said quickly.

"About your writing. Or anything at all," I said. "I'm not in any hurry tonight if you—"

"Next week perhaps," she called over her shoulder, going away. And with a little wave went out the door.

I knew she did not want to talk to me about writing. She came next week and every week. But as always, without a word to me, she escaped like a shadow from the room.

Sometimes, as now, when some bore like Mrs. Hennessey was reading, I caught her watching me furtively. And, as now, I gave her a little twist of a smile. She did not look away, but stared unblinking, pretending not to notice.

I glanced again at my watch. It was eight minutes before nine. Mrs. Hennessey caught the movement, stopped, fluttered her eyes, cleared her throat.

"Shall I go on?" she said. "Or is it time?"

"On and on, by all means," I said. "It's the last night, you know."

"I have only six more tiny pages," she answered. And, over a faint chorus of sighs, cleared her throat again and continued.

She might have gone on into summer. But at that moment the hall door opened and Paul Ferris tiptoed to my desk. He is not at all a solemn type, but his face was grave.

"Couple of men out in the hall want to see you right away, Ross," he said.

"Won't it wait?" I whispered above the drone of Mrs. Hennessey, who had looked up, paused, droned on.

Ferris shook his head.

"Who are they, Paul?"

He came close to my ear. "Detectives," he answered.

I followed him outside, closing the door. They both wore gray suits of differing shades. They were middle-aged. The plump one with the craggy face and the shrewd eyes could have passed for a used-car salesman; the tall one with the glasses, for a CPA.

Their names were mumbled and I did not catch them, indifferent to everything but their purpose.

"We'd like a word with one of your students," said the plump one hoarsely. He seemed a little embarrassed, as if the surroundings intimidated him.

"The class will be out in a few minutes, officer," I said. "Can it wait?"

"No, sir, it can't." Of this he seemed certain.

"Which student, then?"

"A Miss Erickson."

"Erickson? Not in my class, officer."

"Oh, yes, sir," he said vehemently. "In your class, sir."

"Do you know her on sight?"

"I would, yes, sir."

I opened the door slightly, enough for him to scan the room. His eyes moved around slowly from desk to desk and stopped. He lifted his arm and cocked a pudgy finger.

"That's her," he said, pointing at Barbara Dawson in her corner.

"You must be mistaken," I said. I knew he wasn't. I had known all along. Intuitively.

"No, sir," he said. "I'm not mistaken. I'm positive." He nodded. "That's Barbara Erickson."

"And you only want to speak to her a moment, is that it?"

"No, sir, not exactly. I have a warrant for her arrest." I glanced at Paul Ferris. He was chewing his lip, his eyes on his shoes. I felt an unreasoning clutch of despair.

"What's the charge?" I asked. "Can you tell me that much?"

"Yes, sir," he answered. "I sure can." He said it with a kind of perverse pleasure.

"Well?"

"Homicide. She's wanted on suspicion of murder."

CHAPTER 2

I stood out in the hall talking to Paul Ferris. He knew no more about it than I did. Barbara Erickson—that proved to be her legal name—had been taken aside by the officers. They spoke in low tones, and I could not hear what was said.

The class had gone. I had dismissed it immediately with the vague explanation that it was nearly nine anyway and something had come up which made it necessary for me to leave. I wished them all a good summer and said I expected to see many of the same faces in the fall.

I felt a certain official obligation to Barbara Erickson. And of course I had a natural curiosity. There was in me also a sense of pity, however unfounded. And some stronger emotion I couldn't have understood at the time.

After a minute she moved away from the officers and came up to where we were standing. Her face was composed but her voice was strained when she said, "Could I talk with you privately please, Mr. Elliot?"

"Sure," I said, and looked at Paul. He muttered something about calling him if he could help and strode away to his office.

"I need a friend," she said quickly, the second he had gone.

"You've got one then," I answered.

Her hand fluttered to my sleeve in a pathetic little gesture of appreciation.

"I have no friends," she said. "There are just people that I know. It's my fault in a way. But there isn't time to tell you anything much. So please don't ask questions, just listen. My real name is Barbara Erickson. Someone has made a fantastic accusation against me, some jealous love-sick idiot."

"Vandiver?"

She nodded. "He looks harmless but he's a kind of little-boy maniac. He has this insane attachment for me. I brushed him and he's figured out this warped, this simply awful revenge. He's accused me of—of a murder. Something that happened months ago. Yes, I know it's shocking, but I can't explain now."

She looked toward the detectives. They had moved closer and were watching her with growing impatience.

"What can I do to help?" I asked.

"They're going to take me in for questioning," she said. "They may try to hold me in jail. I don't know. First thing, call my lawyer for me. His name is Spencer—Stanford Spencer. His home number is in the book. A maid will answer, and if he's not there, she should be able to locate him. Keep trying. All right.?"

"Right. I'll find him."

"I'll be over at the West L.A. station on Santa Monica Boulevard. Tell him I said to come right down and bail me out."

"Don't you worry. It's done. Anything else?"

"Just stand by. Later, when they let me go, I'll need someone. I'll want to talk and talk. I meant to tell you everything that night long ago. But somehow I—I couldn't."

"Just one question."

"Yes?"

"Why me?"

"Not now," she said. "I'll call you."

"You don't know my number."

"Yes, I do. I almost phoned you once before. In the middle of the night. I looked it up. Ross Elliot, 722 Summit View Drive. Later then. Good-bye."

She kissed me on the cheek and I watched her walk away, receding down the hall between the two officers.

* * * *

Stanford Spencer wasn't at home. The maid told me he had gone to a dinner party. When I said it was an emergency, she gave me a number to call. Someone at the party got Spencer to the phone. He had a cool, testy sound. Until I mentioned that I was calling for Barbara Erickson. The name was a password. It opened him right up.

"Now let me get this straight," he said. "Your name is Ross Elliot and you say that Barbara is in trouble and asked you to call. Why didn't she call herself, Mr. Elliot?"

"She was arrested and taken to the West L.A. police station."

"I see." He didn't sound surprised. "Was there a warrant?"

"They said so. The detectives."

"What was the charge?"

"Suspicion of murder. Homicide, as they call it."

"Christ!" he said. "I wish the whole goddam thing had come to trial. We'd have gotten an acquittal and then they'd have had to leave her alone. Well, I'll hop over there and get her out one way or another, even if I have to light a fire under Judge Boyd. I imagine they just want to question her again."

"It has something to do with Larry Vandiver," I said. "He's made an accusation."

"Oh, Jesus God, the silly bastard. The police will believe anyone when they're hungry. Well, I'll take care of it right away. Thanks for calling, Elliot."

"I hate to sound stupid, Mr. Spencer, but I know nothing of Barbara Erickson in a personal way. What's it all about?"

"My God, don't you get a newspaper?"

"Yes, and I admit the name sounds familiar. But there are lots of Ericksons."

"There was only one Harvey Erickson, my friend. He was her father."

"I still don't—"

"Back in October. Erickson and his wife were just leaving for a night club. It was their anniversary. They got in their car and after that no one knows exactly what happened. Someone gave them a little present. Either they were carrying it or it was left in the car on the seat. They sat there and they opened it. It blew their heads off, my friend. Remember?"

I did. I remember then. Though it was just another of the daily sensations and the details were hazy.

"Yes, I remember now," I said.

"Sure you do. They suspected Barbara because they found the scrap of an anniversary card with her writing on it. To say nothing of the fact that she came into over a million. They never could prove anything. There wasn't enough for an indictment. But I've got to open some doors, Mr. Elliot. You get the rest from her. Okay?"

There was a click and he was gone.

I drove home then to wait. I lived at that time in an apartment house north of Sunset, overlooking the campus of UCLA. It was a small place. I had a ground-floor apartment with a tiny living room and a single bedroom. There were two entrances— the back door opened from the kitchen onto a community patio and grassy back yard, complete with hedge and flowers, a glider and sundry outdoor furniture.

I set the phone with its long cord near the kitchen door and went outside to the glider. For a long time I rocked in the darkness, sipping a highball and smoking. I made another drink and smoked more cigarettes. I came in about ten-thirty and, carrying the phone to the night table, sank upon the bed with a book. I couldn't concentrate. My mind kept falling from the lines into a dreamy sort of speculation. I saw Barbara again, in various attitudes as she sat in class. I saw the detective pointing that accusing finger at her. I felt her hand on my sleeve, the scent of her perfume returned, she kissed me. This time on the mouth. It wasn't quite right. It didn't go with her remoteness.

I saw her hands tying a package. A small package, but heavy. She fastened it and, with a grim expression, slid the card beneath the bow. She placed it on the seat of a car. Nodding, her face became sly and evil. She moved off into the darkness. This too seemed a false picture. I went back to my reading.

The phone rang near eleven-thirty. I dropped the book and grabbed it.

"Mr. Elliot?" she said.

"Ross," I answered.

"Thanks for calling Stan Spencer," she said. "Ross?"

"Yes."

"I'm home. They asked a thousand questions but they couldn't hold me. Will you come over?"

Her voice had a new sound. Tense but intimate. Intimate hysteria.

"Where do you live, Barbara?"

She gave me an address in Beverly Hills. I never believed she lived at some hotel in Hollywood. A hotel room couldn't contain her for long.

"About ten minutes," I said.

"Oh, good, good!" she came back breathlessly. "Please hurry."

I hung up.

* * * *

It was a small split-level house set on one of those cloistered streets behind the Beverly Hills Hotel on Sunset. A yellow light glowed above the door. I could see no other. I went up the walk hesitantly. There was the deep probing growl of a dog. I had the first feeling of being misplaced, out of step with my environment. Of course it was the darkened house, uninviting as the dog.

I saw him, the dog, just inside the screen. An immense Doberman, drawn back on his haunches, poised as an arrow. He murmured a gutturel warning and fanged the darkness with a gleaming grimace.

"Who is it?"

Barbara's voice beyond, edgy as the challenge of an outpost sentry. I saw the firefly of her cigarette.

"It's Dracula," I said. "Who did you expect at this time of night?"

She came floating to the door, a pale outline behind the screen.

"It isn't the people I expect that worry me," she said. "Sorry, Ross. Wait just a moment while I remove the beast. He bites his enemies and has no friends."

She called the dog and they disappeared. A lamp glowed and I saw that she was dressed in a turquoise suit, a wool knit that hugged every hill and valley of her magnificent terrain.

She unlatched the screen, a taint of apology in her smile. I stepped inside and now she closed the door, bolting it, setting the chain.

The living room was Danish modern, cool arid lines softened with rich fabrics and islands of color.

"I'm renting for the time being," she said. "The decor is inherited from the owner."

"It shames the best room in a Hollywood hotel," I said.

She frowned. "I stayed in that hotel just three days," she said. "Until I found this. There aren't half a dozen people who know exacly where I live. And now you're one of them. Try that big chair by the ottoman. You'll love it. Drink?"

"You have some bourbon?"

"And a little soda?"

"A little soda. Very little."

She brought a dark one to my chair and carried her own to the sofa where she assembled herself against the pillows without managing to look comfortable, merely coiled. And tense.

"Do you really like that monster, Barbara? The one who has no friends?"

"Grizz?"

"Is that his name? Grizz?"

"As in grizzly bear."

"Why don't you just call him 'Horrible'? For short."

She laughed. Without joy. "He's better than a gun. And noisier."

She plucked a cigarette from a jeweled silver box on the coffee table. She waved me off and took flame from the figurine lighter beside the box.

"Did Stan tell you anything about me?"

"Stan?"

"Stanford Spencer."

"Oh, the lawyer. Yes, a little. It never occurred to me that I was *that* Erickson?"

"Yes."

"I was there when it happened, you know," she said quickly, exhaling furiously and picking a shard of tobacco from the tip of her tongue. "I had a date. I was in the living room waiting for him, reading the paper. I was early. I never dress at the last minute and keep someone fidgeting around as if I didn't want to go in the first place. That's silly. I mean, if you don't want to do a thing, say so. But don't play coy by delaying and pretending you're a little bored with it all. Isn't that right?"

"What? Oh, sure. The honest approach," I answered, too casually.

She gazed at me blankly. I was afraid she wouldn't go on.

"It was their anniversary," she said finally. "Mother and dad's. Not my real mother, my stepmother Phyllis. Anyway, it was their anniversary. They were going to celebrate at some club on the Strip. I forget now. And they came downstairs all dressed up and…and kissed me good-bye. We had a butler who was also a chauffeur, but dad seldom used him. He liked to drive himself. The car, a gray Cadillac, had already been backed from the garage. It was in the driveway.

"I heard the front door close and after that nothing else I remember. Not even the car starting. Just the other—the big sound. Loud—oh, yes, of course. But muffled, too. And weirdly evil.

"I had no idea what it was. I ran out the door, down the steps. I saw the car smoking. You would have thought… But it wasn't so badly damaged. From a distance it looked almost all right. I remember wondering if the motor could have, if something could have… But anyway, I ran over. And I looked in.

"Ross, I want you to know that was a big mistake. Looking in that window. But how could I have guessed? How *could* I! I won't think of it for days, even a week now. And then the dirty thing, that obscene picture, will come like a—like a filthy bat, fluttering and drifting up from my subconscious. I can be reading, or just walking down the street. Or I can wake up in the middle of the night and feel it coming. Insidious.

No building a wall to hide it either. No closing the eyes." She tapped her head. "Not these eyes up here. In the mind. They never close." She swallowed. "Never," she whispered.

I didn't say anything. I couldn't.

She took a long drink. I watched the pulse of her throat.

"The map light," she said. "Isn't that what you call it? Yes. Well, it was still on. Can you believe it? Still on! They must have found the package on the seat. I'm quite sure they weren't carrying anything. So they found it on the seat and they turned on the light. And they must have both been bent down over it when it exploded." She paused. "The rest is too grotesque, too obscene to tell you. Obscene, obscene!"

She gave a wry little smile. "I have to speak of it in a kind of flat, objective way, you see, Ross. Forgive me. But anything more is overboard into—well, into something you wouldn't want to see."

"I understand that perfectly, Barbara." I cleared my throat, stared into the glass, jiggling ice.

"And of course it isn't over," she said, leaning towards me with a fixed expression. "It can just be forgotten, if that were ever possible. Because out there somewhere there's a man or a woman still free to do it again." She sank back with a sigh.

"Do you wonder that I'm careful? Do you wonder that I'm a little nervous? Do you, Ross?"

CHAPTER 3

Barbara went into the kitchen to make us another drink. Distantly I heard her voice. She was speaking in a kind of monotone. Mechanical. Singsong. At first I was bewildered.

Then I realized that she was chanting to the dog. I suppose Grizz was soothed by the usual baby-talk. But he hardly seemed the type.

Carrying the drinks, slender fingers curled around the glasses, Barbara came towards me across the room. She moved gracefully and without the sexy undulations of uncertain females who have to advertise. I watched the ebony sway of her hair where it looped below the nape of her neck. When she smiled and passed the drink, I decided she was not really cold. Just defensive. And for all her remote and secretive ways in class, she had an almost blunt sincerity. Did sincere people kill? Sincerely?

The fresh drink seemed nearly all bourbon.

"This one has more teeth than Grizz, Barbara. Trying to get me drunk?"

She sat down, kicking off her shoes, stretching her legs. "Not drunk, Ross. Just easy and relaxed. I can see how all this would make you slightly uncomfortable. Now that you know, I must appear more freak than human to you. By association." She held up her hand. "Oh, no. It's a perfectly natural reaction. I expected it. And that's why I was never quite brave enough to confide in you. Until those detectives put me on exhibit."

"Why would you *ever* want to confide in me?"

She looked down. "That's a rather embarrassing question. I'll skirt around it for the time being. I did read a couple of your books." She looked up again. "They were good stories. And more. They showed insight. And they were sensitive. Oh, God, how sensitive! I can't talk to insensitive people who have alligator hides around one or two feeble emotions. And have pale responses to about four basics—heat, cold, food and sex. They nod and make the right faces. But for all their awareness you might as well be speaking Chinese with a mouth full of molasses. I can't talk to people like that. Not any more. I'd rather be alone. Does that explain anything?"

"Quite a lot."

"I read your books, and then when I saw that item in the paper saying you were going to conduct the writing class,—well, I was more than curious. So I registered. But I just couldn't seem to crawl out of myself. My safe anonymity. The police had been haunting me, reporters tailing me, my so-called friends studying me like something on a lab slide. Then there were family problems—jealously, suspicion, bickering over dad's will. All done with saccharine words and smiles and phony droolings about grief.

"I had to escape. I rented this house without a word to anyone but Stan Spencer, who forwards my mail, and Larry Vandiver. I needed Larry. He seemed harmless. And Platonic. But he turned into something else entirely."

"Tell me about him. Vandiver."

She got another cigarette from the box and lighted it. She tucked her legs beneath her.

"Larry and I went to college together. I mean, we met at college and discovered we lived a few blocks from each other. I liked him. Not physically. Biologically, he just wasn't there for me. I set him straight on that and he went right along with it docilely enough. And I thought, My God, here's one you can just talk to without practicing your jujitsu. In fact, it got so cozy I told him about some of my little pseudoromances and he fed me the same kind of thing back.

"It was all buddy-buddy and continued that way after college. Sometimes we even went out with different people together. Larry is no deep brain but he can communicate and he has, or pretends to have, a certain sympathy and understanding that is comforting. It used to be.

"Then this—this thing happened to my parents. Next day, Larry was right over there with his big Platonic arm around me, and he was just the sort I needed. No involvements—just a towel and a pair of shoulders. So when I decided to disappear, he was one of the few I trusted. He used to come over here two or three times a week and he got to be a sort of husband without portfolio. I depended on him.

"Then a week went by and I didn't see him. He was on a fishing trip to Encenada. I was miserable. I was so lonely and depressed that when he came in the door I kissed him as if he were the great lover returning. He misunderstood and I was too empty to resist much. I let him go a little too far. By the time I got around to fighting him off, it was too late. Suddenly he just went crazy. Out of control. One minute he was telling me about this tortured love he had for me; the next he was holding me by the throat and tearing my clothes off. He was choking me to death and didn't even know it.

"I had Grizz tied up in the kitchen but the door was open. He heard me, snapped his leash like it was paper and came bounding in. He leaped on Larry and would have killed him if I hadn't called him off. Larry was so apologetic, I forgave him. But he had changed. Or at least he had come out into the open with his grand passion. And everywhere that Barbara went, Larry was sure to follow. He got to pawing me again that same night he made a fool of me in class. I was fed up anyway. I ordered him out of the house and told him not to come back. Ever."

"You didn't hear from him again?" I asked.

"Not exactly. The phone rang half a dozen times. When I answered, there was someone on the line who wouldn't speak. It must have been Larry. The number's unlisted. A couple of nights I looked out the window and saw him watching the house from across the street. I wanted to call the police but I don't exactly consider them friends."

"Now there's a twist. In the end he went to the police himself. What did he say, Barbara? That is, if you feel like telling me."

She was silent, staring at her nails. She got up and padded across the room to a window. She parted the drape and looked out. She turned.

"I'm just stalling," she said. "Everything Larry said is a lie. But it's such a filthy, evil lie."

"Don't tell it then. Unless you have a compulsion to talk about it. Unless it gives you relief, I mean."

She came back and sat down. She took a deep breath and squeezed her eyes shut.

"He said I killed dad and Phyllis." She opened her eyes. "There!" she said.

"Well, that's about what I expected, Barbara."

"Did you expect him to say that I planned the whole thing a long time ago and asked him to help me?"

"No."

"Of course, he also said that he refused, and that I said I would get someone else to help me make a bomb."

"Did he offer any reason why he didn't go to the police before?"

"Oh, certainly. He didn't believe me. He thought I was just angry and would get over it. Angry because dad wouldn't give me money to go abroad and live for a couple of years. Angry at dad and furious with Phillis because she was getting twice the attention and ten times the money. Looking back, said Larry, he could see I had these resentments, to say nothing of my inheritance, as motives. But at the time he didn't think me capable of such a crime and was sure I was just blowing off steam. Then, after it happened, he knew I did it. But he was afraid to come forward. He might get involved. He might be a suspect himself, be held in jail for trial. He couldn't stand that. But our hero had a conscience and at last it got the better of him. He was simply compelled to tell the truth."

"Great. And did our hero explain why, if he was so shocked at your crime, he spent more time than ever with you?"

"Oh, yes, of course. He had an answer for everything. He played up to me in order to pump me for information he could use against me. Sadly, he was unsuccessful."

"He's been thinking about this a long time then," I said. "It was well planned and rehearsed. I don't see how you got free, even with Spencer's help."

"Well, because as Stan said, an accusation isn't evidence. Larry had nothing concrete, not even a witness. All he did was stir up more trouble and suspicion. The police wanted to un-nerve me with Larry and get a confession. When it didn't work, they had to let me go. But now the police know where I live and they'll be watching me night and day. Oh, God, I'm so tired, Ross, so terribly tired of living with this tension."

"Do you think it's possible that Vandiver did it himself, Barbara?"

She mashed her cigarette, said to the tray, "You haven't asked me if I did it, Ross."

"That means you want me to ask so you can say no, you didn't do it. All right, I believe you. Let's pass on to other things."

"Thanks," she said. And her eyes were moist. "As for Larry, I don't think so. Where's his motive? He had nothing to gain. Certainly not me or any part of my money."

"Who does that leave, then?"

"Oh, dear God, any number of people. My father had a partner, Donald Huffman. Together they owned a chain of su-permarkets, you may remember. The Quick Shop places. The contract stipulated that, after certain financial arrangements, the business must go to the surviving partner. Well, if Mr. Huffman wanted to get control…

"And then there's my uncle, my father's brother. He stood to gain in the will. And my stepsister Lois, who lives in New York. And Stan Spencer, who is executor and knows more about Dad's finances than anyone. And some—uh—girl friend or mistress. My father was only forty-six, good looking, and a little too generous with his affections. His charities began at home but had no boundaries. So, a jealous woman… And then, of course, he had his enemies like anyone else in control of a big enterprise. The possibilities are infinite."

"Anyone you suspect in particular?"

She shook her head. "These are just people with motive. I have no real reason to suspect any of them. I haven't a single clue. In fact, the only clue the police found pointed right to me. The anniversary card. A scrap of one. My handwriting was on it."

"Your handwriting or a forgery?"

"My handwriting. No doubt about it. And yet I didn't even write a card. The fact is, I didn't even give them a present. I forgot. No, I didn't forget really. I didn't want to give them anything. I had my reasons. I forgot on purpose. But the car thing frightens me. It scares me every time I think of it. Someone can imitate my handwriting so well, I can't tell the difference myself. Imagine the damage a person like that can do! Oh, let's not talk about it any more tonight, Ross. I'll just work myself into another state. Your glass is empty. Drink?"

"No thanks. It's late. I'd better go." I stood up.

She followed me to the door. She caught my arm and squeezed. "I'm grateful," she said. "It was getting to be too much for me. If you hadn't come… Anyway, thanks."

"For nothing," I said, and reached for the door. Then, on impulse, I leaned down and kissed her. It was intended to be a quick gesture. But her arms came around me and she held on. Her mouth opened, she pressed against me. And that was when I knew I was in deep. And all the way. My hand wound up her side and closed over her breast.

"Don't go," she whimpered. "Don't go."

"All right." I stroked her hair. "All right, I won't go."

"No," she said quickly. "You'd better go."

"But you just said—"

"It's the wrong time. In this mood, it's a dangerous time."

"What kind of danger?"

"You know what kind."

"The kind I like."

"Go now. But come back."

"Tomorrow?"

"Tomorrow."

I went out. Knowing that I had been drawn long ago to the girl in my class who had called herself Barbara Dawson. And was in love with Barbara Erickson.

CHAPTER 4

In a kind of rapture I went down the walk to my car. Those last moments with Barbara still clung to me. It was after 1:00 A.M. and the houses in the block hunched in shadow and slept. Royal palms rammed themselves skyward, faced each other across the street in orderly ranks, wore gray-white uniforms and green plume hats. The silence had a depth born of the hour and of suburban isolation.

I looked back once. But Barbara's house was already dark. Was she watching me from a window? I had a feeling of dream-like detachment, as if I moved within myself, my surroundings unreal. I approached my car. A street lamp made a small pool of light on the rear deck. I reached with my key toward the door lock.

The bullet struck the curb at my feet and sang away. The other sound was no more than a puff, like that of an air gun. Or a silencer. For a moment I stood paralyzed. Then I threw myself to the ground.

The second shot struck the side of the car above me. I had a hazy confused impression that both sound and trajectory had come from the direction of Barbara's house. I crawled out of the light, around the car to the passenger door. I reached up with the key and got it open. I hoisted myself in. Shutting the door quietly behind me, I lay flat across the seat, trying to get the key in the ignition lock with a shaky hand. I got a foot on the accelerator, turned the key. The motor caught; I slipped the gear shift into drive and the car leaped ahead. If there was another shot I didn't hear the bullet strike. I drove without lights and didn't sit up fully until I reached the next corner. I hadn't a single conscious thought but flight until I reached Sunset. Then I remembered the headlights, opened the windows and gulped air.

I was alone on the boulevard. I could see no one following me. My mind began to function and I realized that I had made a wrong turn if I was going home. Was I? I was. To go back was ridiculous. To get the police made more sense. But I could call them from my apartment. And I could use the ride to think. I turned around.

By the time I reached my place I had decided not to call the police. What would I tell them? That someone shot at me? Who? And from where? From Barbara Erickson's house, officer. Well, not exactly from her house, of course. But very nearby. That would toss Barbara a curve, now wouldn't it? The police would love to find an excuse to take her in again. No, I would phone her a warning.

I admit the direction from which the shot seemed to have come put a small doubt in my mind. But why should Barbara... Absurd. In fact, why should anyone at all want to kill me? Probably I had been mistaken for someone else. But it was a dangerous mistake. And for a short space there Barbara didn't seem quite so fascinating.

I parked the car on the street in front of my building. I got out and flamed my lighter, searching along the driver's side. I found the place—a small oblique hole in the lower section of the door. I ran my finger over it, picturing that same hole in my back. Apparently, from the look of it, the shot had been fired from above. Since an air rifle or pellet gun would not have the velocity for such penetration, that left a pistol or a rifle with a silencer. A silencer makes you think of both planning and the professional touch. It made me think how pleasant those dull, routine summers were after all.

I went inside and made a very strong drink. I was taking it to the phone when I remembered that Barbara had an unlisted number. And that was a problem. I took off my coat and sat down to figure it when there was a light tap at my back door. I listened and heard it again.

I set the drink on the kitchen table. I went to the door and looked out through the glass. I could see nothing, so I flipped on the outside light. Still nothing. I opened the door and stepped out cautiously. The glider caught my eye. It was swaying slightly. I went toward it, stopped. Below, ground into the grass, were three cigarette stubs. One was still smoking. Someone had been sitting there at least a half-hour. I was looking into the shadows beyond the glider when I heard the soft quick pad of footsteps behind me.

I whirled. Just in time to catch the bone sledge of a fist on the side of my jaw. I gave with the blow, stepping backward and dancing aside. A nearly silent gun fired from some secret place was one thing. But this kind of enemy I understood.

He was a big guy, about my size. I recognized him. It was Vandiver. He came in strong, charging. He was full of steam and muscle but he had no skill. He bounced one off my temple. I sidestepped and clobbered him across the side of the face, under the eye. He staggered, swinging blindly. I followed the advantage, ramming his nose, battering his mouth, delivering the best one to his jaw.

He went down, got to his knees and couldn't rise. I wanted to hit him again because I hated the lying bastard. But instead I gave him a shove with my foot that spread him out gasping on his back. I watched him a moment—watched the blood drooling from his nose into his open mouth, coursing down his chin onto his shirt. Then I grabbed his hair and pulled him into a sitting position. I cocked a fist.

"On your feet, mister," I said. "Or you'll wake up in the hospital."

He got his legs under him and stood, slouching. He swayed like a drunk. I opened the door and pushed him inside. I walked him to a chair by a lamp. "Okay. Down!"

He sat. I stood over him, working my bruised knuckles. His cut lip began to bleed. He mopped. He blinked and stared his hatred. His eyes were puffed and red, as if he had gone without sleep for a long time.

"Why?" I said.

He didn't answer.

"Just tell me that, Vandiver. Why? Why me?"

"I want you to stay away from her," he said.

"Her?" I knew damn well, of course.

"Barbara. Leave her alone. You and Barbara." He nodded. "I know." He kept nodding. "She never goes home after class any more. She comes here with you. I know. Don't go near her. Don't touch her again." His hands tightened on the arm rests. "You hear? Don't touch her! I'm warning you, Elliot."

"Every Wednesday night. Is that it?"

"Other times too. She's having—she's—she's—"

"Sleeping with me?"

"Shut up! Oh, goddam you shut up!"

I didn't deny it. I wanted to open him up.

"Tell me something, Vandiver. Are you crazy?"

"What?"

"Or are you sick? You play the lover-boy protector. And out of the other side of your mouth you tell lies to the police."

"They're not lies!" he shouted. "It's all true. She—"

"Lies, Vandiver. Lies." I leaned forward, stared into his face. "You want to send Barbara to the gas chamber? Is that what you want? Answer me, you sonofabitch! Is that what you want?"

Slowly his face compressed, squeezed itself out of shape. A tear ran from one bloodshot eye. He lowered his head and made a small sobbing sound.

"They wouldn't—they wouldn't kill her," he said. "Not Barbara. She has money for the best lawyers in the world. A couple of years in jail, maybe five. Not over five." He wiped his eyes, looking up. "And while she's there, no one cancan touch her. Not even you. Then when she gets out I'll be waiting, don't you see? They'll take that money away from her. It's the law. And she won't have anything or anyone. Only me. Don't you get it, Elliot? My God, don't you understand?"

"Sure," I said, and gave him a hard open hand across the

face. "Sure, Vandiver, I understand perfectly. You want to crucify her, you filthy bastard. And then when they take her down off the cross, you'll collect the body."

He looked at me with hurt amazement.

"You still don't get it," he said. "She really did it." He added monotonously. "She blew Phyllis and her father to bits that night. Her father was sitting there with one hand on the wheel like he was driving—only he didn't have any head. I know she did it because she asked me to help get rid of them and I told her how it could be done. Then at the last minute I backed out, and she got someone else."

I studied him carefully. And the odd part of it was, I think he really believed it. He had gone over it so much he had convinced himself. He seemed a nut. Hopeless. He was in a kind of self-made stupor, and I decided to play along, leading him to a new subject.

"Well," I said. "Of course this all happened before I knew Barbara. You might be telling the truth."

"The truth," he said. "That's right. Only the truth."

"Sure, Larry. The truth. So all you really want to do is help Barbara."

He brightened. "Yes, that's all. I can help Barbara, if she'd let me. Why don't you talk to her, Mr. Elliot?"

Now it was *mister*. "Oh, I will, Larry, I will talk to her. But now about tonight. You were under a strain, worried about barbara. So you came over here to—uh—persuade me to leave her alone."

"Yes. I didn't mean any harm. Really."

"But before that, before you came here, where were you?"

"At the police station. Until about eleven. They were questioning me again. And Barbara, she—"

"So aroung eleven you left the station. Where did you go?"

"Why?"

"Is there anything to hide? Now?"

"Well, I had a couple of drinks at a bar and then I drove over to Barbara's house. About a quarter of twelve. I knew they had released her and I wanted to talk to her. But then I saw a car in front. I parked up the block and walked back. I looked in a window and I saw it was you."

"So then you got the gun with the silencer and you hid somewhere on the grounds and waited for me to come out. Right?"

"Gun? What gun? What silencer?" He looked thoroughly puzzled.

"Never mind. What *did* you do?"

"I just sat in the car for about fifteen minutes, stewing. I was all mixed up. Then I went home. I lay on the bed in the dark with my clothes on, thinking some more. Then I left and came over here to wait for you."

"What time was that?"

"Around twelve-thirty or so. Why all the questions?"

"You went out back and sat in the glider?"

"Yes."

"How long were you there?"

"I dunno. Three-quarters of an hour or more, I guess."

The way he told it, cigarette butts on the grass and all, it seemed logical. I didn't like it. That left someone else with the gun. You take one small step into a situation and how many people can want you out of the way before you even understand what it's all about?

"All right," I said. "Let's take a walk."

"Where?"

"To your car. Come on—up!"

I followed him out to the street. He had parked the Chevvy around the corner. I checked the interior. The glove compartment was locked and I made him open it. A pair of sun glasses and a dust cloth. The trunk contained only the spare and tools.

"Okay, Vandiver. Beat it. Take off!"

He climbed behind the wheel and I leaned in the window. "Don't come back, either. I catch you within a mile of here or Barbara's house, I'll chop you in much finer pieces before I turn you over to the police."

He started the car, gave me a long sullen look and gunned off. I watched his taillights fade around a corner. Then I went back inside and made another drink.

CHAPTER 5

It was nearly four o'clock in the morning. I couldn't sleep. I hadn't even undressed. I lay on the bed and tried to read. I couldn't do that either. I was nervous. Hell, I was more than nervous. I was frightened. If someone is determined to kill you, they will do it one way or another. And I wouldn't even have the dubious satisfaction of knowing why before it happened. Although being shot at and ambushed in my own back yard were not exactly routine before I met Barbara.

But I was also full of anger and rebellion. Because in effect I was being told to stay away from Barbara, have nothing to do with her. And suddenly I wanted to have a lot to do with Barbara. A whole lot. Pride and desire wouldn't let me scare off. I accepted the whole thing as a challenge.

I put the book down finally and undressed. I cut the light and got into bed. Twenty minutes later the light was on again. And so were my clothes. I got the box down from my closet shelf. It had been so long since I had looked inside it, I had almost forgotten it was there. I opened it, took the rubberband off the oily rag and unwound it from the gun. It was a .22 revolver, a target pistol. I didn't use it twice a year and had threatened to sell it but never got around to making the effort. The barrel was too long for a concealed weapon but the gun would fit in the glove compartment and it was more accurate than those stubby jobs. And don't let anyone tell you a .22 is little better than a toy. A well placed .22 contains just as much permanent sleep as any other bullet.

I got the little cleaning rod, inserted a patch in the eye tip and drove it back and forth in the oily barrel. I cleaned the cylinder chambers, wiped the exterior surface of the gun and began to load it from a box of cartridges.

At that moment the doorbell rang.

Quickly I finished loading, snapped the cylinder in place and carried the gun to the door. The fact that someone came around front and rang didn't seem reassuring. It was a quarter after four and the whole night read like something out of a police file.

For seconds I listened at the door. Then I called, "Who is it?"

There was no reply, so I called again. Louder.

The answer came half-spoken, half-whispered.

"It's me, Ross. Barbara!"

I opened and she soft-shoed rapidly into the room, holding her breath until I had locked the door. She had on a gold sweater with a black crest and wore a tight black skirt. It was a smart combination. Still, I had the impression she had dressed in a hurry.

"I didn't want to wake everyone in the building," she said. "What are you doing with that gun?"

"It's been that kind of a night."

She stared at the weapon with extreme distaste.

"I loathe guns," she said. "Please, Ross, put it away."

I set the .22 on an end table and waited. She moved about the room looking at everything, seeing nothing. She seemed deeply upset while making an enormous effort to conceal it.

"Trouble?" I said.

"Not really. Could you make us a drink?"

"Not really? Then why are you here at four in the morning?"

"Why are you dressed? And why did you have a gun in your hand?"

"I'll make that drink," I said.

I looked back from the kitchen doorway. She had dropped to the sofa. She was hunched over, hugging herself, biting her lip. I made the drinks strong and returned. She drank deeply and gave me a nervous smile.

"Have you got a lot of this stuff?"

"All you want."

"I'm going to want."

I sat down beside her. I took a long drink. I felt relieved. Excited that she was there in my apartment. A few hours ago she was almost a stranger. And now I felt as if she was completely woven into my life. I knew she brought trouble and a whole complex of violent emotions. I didn't care. She had taken another step closer to me. I wanted that. My God, how I wanted it. I rested my arm lightly across her shoulder.

"Tell me," I said.

"Oh, it's nothing. I'm just a little girl in the dark. I heard noises downstairs. And all of a sudden I was up to here with panic. I threw on my clothes and ran out."

"What about Grizz? Didn't he bark?"

"Grizz? Well, no, *he* didn't. And that worried me even more. I thought, Oh, God, if I hear it and he doesn't, I'm alone. I have no protection."

"What sort of sounds?"

"I can't describe them accurately. A kind of tearing or ripping. And then a few little taps."

I told her then about Vandiver. I was sure it would twist her that much tighter. But she had to be warned.

"Ross," she said, "listen to me." She took my hands in hers. "I don't know who shot at you. But I do know this. It couldn't have been personal. You're only in danger while you're around me. And I'm being utterly selfish. You ought to stay away from me until somehow this—this maniac, whoever he is, gets caught." She made a bitter little sound. "I don't know how he'll be caught because the police are convinced that *I'm* the maniac. But I'm just as selfish in asking you to help me long distance until this is over. Because I don't want anything to happen to you."

"Thanks. But, Barbara, I—"

"It's a contradiction, Ross. You're just the one I need, because you never were involved even remotely. And I trust you. But go back to your own quiet little life and forget me."

"No."

"You won't?"

"Get a restraining order."

"You absolutely won't leave me alone?"

"No."

"Then for God's sake help me, Ross. Help me," she sobbed. "Help me, help me!"

I held her and waited until the last little gasp had died.

"Now," I said, "what can I do?"

"Make me another drink." She wiped her eyes, smiled frantically and giggled in a kind of hysterical relief. "Yes," she said, "that's what you can do. Make me another drink."

After I had brought it and she had gulped about half, her mood changed abruptly. "Ross," she said, "are you always so gallant? I mean, would you do this for someone else? Just anyone in trouble?"

"Don't be silly. Of course not. I have very personal and selfish reasons. I help blind men across the street and I pick up old ladies who stumble. Otherwise, I have no altruistic tendencies."

"Tell me about these personal reasons," she teased.

"I don't have to. You know very well. It's probably written all over me."

She put down her drink. Her face grew serious again. "I knew there would be something between us long before you did," she said. "I knew it the first night I walked into your classroom. But I couldn't force it. It had to come about in its own way. And now what shall we call it? Love? Or animal magnetism?"

"It starts with one and sometimes becomes the other," I said. "Sometimes. And if you're very lucky, it remains a mixture of both."

"But it starts with that hungry animal, doesn't it?"

"Let's not kid ourselves."

"And then it turns into love? You separate love from sex?"

"Yes. They blend but they're not the same. Love is too big

a word for sex. Because sex is narrow, limited, and essentially selfish. If that sounds idealistic, don't be fooled. I have my very narrow, limited, and essentially selfish side. It's the one facing you right now."

She chuckled, gave me a delighted smile which, when it was gone, left her face painfully sad and wanting.

"I don't care a hoot about definitions right now," she said. "I don't want to pull the wings off my emotions with too much probing. I have more than a million dollars and it hasn't yet given me a happy day. But whatever *you* call it, and whatever it becomes, for now I need you, for now I love you."

Well, naturally I kissed her. And naturally I told her I loved her too. And no longer gave a damn about definitions either. And I got the sweater up and the other things down, hating the awkward delays of clothing. She sat naked to the waist and her breasts pushed upward out of shadow into the soft hem of light from the lamp. And when I touched in the shadows she said, "You have lover's hands." And when I kissed where the light fell she murmured, "And a lover's mouth. But I'm afraid of men who know too much about making love. I need affection, too. Oh, Ross, if you can't give me that, stop now. Stop now!"

But I didn't stop. And I gave her that affection. Later. As we lay naked and content in my bed. Then the tension of the night drained out of me. And just before dawn I fell asleep.

CHAPTER 6

I came awake sometime after eleven in the morning. I was alone in the bed and thought I had been dreaming. But the impression of her head was there on the pillow with a tiny smear of lipstick. And faintly, the scent of her was in the room.

There was a soot-gray darkness outside the windows. It was raining, the rain driven by gusts of wind, the sky too thick to be broken by clouds. I knew she was not just in another room, but gone. I could feel her absence. I found that depressing. I wanted to be alone with her. It was a perfect day for that rare combination of passion and domesticity.

In spite of my conviction that Barbara was gone, I put on a robe and went through the motions of padding from room to room, a very brief search and pointless. She had left something though. I found an envelope (one of my own) impaled upon the shaft of my desk pen. When I opened it I found a letter written on my stationery, and two checks. Both checks were made out to me. One was for fifty thousand dollars. The other for ten thousand. Since sixty thousand represented about ten years of labor in my bracket, I didn't waste much time hunting the explanation in Barbara's letter. I read it twice.

Ross darling, Please forgive me for stealing away like this while you sleep. And know that I will take last night (this morning?) with me and carry it around in that secret pocket of my mind where I keep the few things I still treasure.

I do think it best now, in this sober (somber?) morning attitude, for me to hold you at a very safe distance. If you still want to help me out of this sordid mess, I'm sure you can do so much better if we remain entirely separate. You'll have twice the freedom. And you'll be out of danger.

Darling, I can't afford to let you take the risk! Against such depravity, such evil. So again, I'm going to vanish. This time where no one could ever find me. Not even you. Especially you, whom I want to find me most.

The police are useless for reasons we both understand. Perhaps the next best thing would be a private detective. Please hire a *good* one for me. Pay him from the ten thousand and use the balance any way you think best.

The fifty thousand is to be used as a reward for "information leading to the arrest and conviction" (isn't that the way they put it?) of the person or persons who murdered my parents. This is a private offer to be made among the people whose names appear below. I can't tell you why, but I know one of them will have all or part of the answer. This was not done by some "outsider." And enough money will open doors and mouths with most of this bunch. In any case, have the detective interview each one and make the offer before we try other avenues. Hold the fifty thousand in your account.

There are reasons why I can't handle this myself. And darling, please don't think I'm a coward for running off. I am, but don't think it. Finally, no matter what you see or hear, please, please trust me and keep faith in me.

I love you! Barbara

P. S. I'll be in touch by phone in a few days.

On a separate sheet was a list of names, a few of which were familiar to me. Beside each name was an address.

I couldn't quite understand why Barbara hadn't told me her plans in person. We could have discussed the details. She must have made the decision before she came over. I was sure of it. Probably, I thought, she was afraid I would try to talk her out of hiding where neither I nor anyone else could reach her. If so, how right she was. I wanted her close. I wanted to keep an eye on her. Now I would worry. Until she called me "in a few days." How vague and uncertain a promise that was.

And she wanted me to trust her, to keep faith. Why? What would I see or hear to give me doubts? On the other hand, her trust in me was little short of naïve. Sixty thousand dollars and instructions, but no strings to keep me honest. A million or no million, this was love!

There was something else, too. About her state of mind when she came to me at four in the morning. The look of her. Frightened. In a state of shock. Close to hysteria. And concealing it with an enormous but unsuccessful effort. I found it difficult to believe that Barbara, with that cool stability she could muster, would react so strongly to just "hearing noises."

I looked again at the checks. Ten thousand for private detectives to ask a few questions and offer a reward. What a waste! I could ask questions and make offers as well as anyone else. And what would it cost me but time and a few gallons of gas? I would take a much more personal interest. I would be thorough. And in a way I would enjoy it—a new experience. Perhaps, I rationalized, Barbara had wanted me to handle it myself all along. She was only afraid to ask. Later, if the results were negative, I could hire detectives to search in some darker corners among professional killers with professional motives. Why not? I wouldn't be sitting around waiting. There would be purpose and direction.

The whole idea gave me sense of satisfaction and excitement. I put the checks in my wallet. I showered and shaved, got dressed quickly and went out.

I deposited both checks in my account at the bank. For once I broke down the bored indifference of a teller. He did a double take, looked again at the checks, raised one eyebrow and smiled broadly when he gave me the receipt. What a busy, frowning little man he would have been if I had asked for cash.

It had stopped raining but the sky was still a solemn promise of more to come. I sat in my car around the corner from the bank and looked at the list of names Barbara had left me. Donald Huffman, Larry Vandiver, Stanford Spencer…Spencer. The lawyer. At least he would know who I was. And he might open some other doors for me. Yes, logically, he should be first.

Spencer's office was on Hill Street in L.A. I took Sunset. It would route me right by the turn-off to Barbara's. And though I had every reason to believe she wouldn't be at home, still there was a chance she had been delayed. I wound into Beverly Hills, swung left and over to her street. I parked in front. Remembering the night before and the hush-voiced evil of that stealthy gun, I had an uncomfortable moment as I went up the walk. But then it was daylight. Of a kind.

All the blinds were drawn. There is something melancholy about a house of lidded eyes in the afternoon. As if the owner has gone on some sad journey, leaving behind only an aura of regret. Though admittedly, Barbara's absence, the distorted shape of her life, gave depth to the mood.

I tried the door. Of course it was locked. I stood there for a time, wondering about Grizz. I might even have welcomed so small a remnant of Barbara as his growl. What had she done with him?

I went around to the back door and it too was locked. Then I noticed the missing section of glass in one of the little frames. And a piece of tape dangling beneath it. I knew how it was done. You cut the glass and you tape the incision; then you tap and the glass comes away neatly and quite silently. That's when you reach in and unlock the door. Which I did then, remembering Barbara's description of those sounds.

Grizz was just inside. He had been shot once in the head and once in the chest. His mouth and eyes were open. Blood covered his muzzle and spread beneath him. He looked smaller, and not at all vicious.

I went back to the car and got the target pistol from the glove compartment. I went through the kitchen into the dark living room. I stood there, wondering if I should draw back the drapes and reveal my presence. I did not know exactly what I would find. But I had made a sickening guess. I walked toward a lamp in the gloom and lighted it.

There were splotches of blood on the rug. I followed their

trail to the stairs and mounted. The lamp cast such a feeble light that I didn't see the body near the top until I was a few feet from it. I stepped over it carefully and found the light switch above.

He had fallen backwards down the stairs and lay with arms and feet outstretched. His head was twisted to one side. I went back down and bent to look.

It was Vandiver. One bullet had gone through his shoulder. But that hadn't stopped him. The way I put it together, he had been shot first down there in the living room. Then he had fled up the stairs and the second shot had scored the back of his head as he reached the top.

I moved through the rest of the rooms in a daze. There was nothing. On the way out, I wiped the door knobs with my handkerchief. I drove all the way to Highland before I stopped at a drugstore and called the police from a booth. When the officer asked my name I hung up.

Then I went to the first bar I could find. I had three drinks in less than ten minutes.

They didn't help at all.

CHAPTER 7

It didn't take long to reason why Barbara had gone into hiding once I knew about Vandiver. It seemed obvious that she had shot him. And that meant she wouldn't be able to talk herself out of jail this time, not even with the best lawyer. Vandiver was an enemy, a witness against her. Dead in her house, he was an accusation beyond denial.

I sat alone in a booth, drinking my fourth more slowly and trying to decide which way to jump. One thing kept me from turning the sixty thousand over to her lawyer and closing Barbara out of my life for keeps. Logically, Vandiver had forced his way in. Barbara didn't cut the glass in her own back door, shoot Grizz herself, then Vandiver. He must have broken in with some frenzied insane purpose—to rape, to kill. Or both. And so she shot him in self-defense. She was justified but she got panicky and she ran.

There was another possibility. Someone else shot Vandiver. While she was with me or on the way to me. The someone else who pumped bullets at me through the mouth of a silencer. Yet Barbara's manner had indicated that she was practically in a state of shock and knew more than she was telling. But it was possible. And I had an obsessive need to believe in her. So I decided to go on a while longer searching for answers. If she knew all the answers herself, would she risk sixty thousand just to convince me she didn't?

I went to a phone at the back of the room and called Stanford Spencer's office. The girl said he was in conference and couldn't be disturbed for anyone. I decided to go there in person and wait.

The office, a three-room suite and reception area, was on the seventh floor of a large building which dominated a busy section of Hill Street. Behind the reception desk a girl produced staccato sounds from an electric typewriter. She looked up. I gave her my name and told her it was urgent. She was unimpressed.

"Mr. Spencer is in conference, sir. I'm sorry, but you might have to wait for some time."

"I'm willing. If you'll just give him my name."

She frowned, shrugged, wrote the name on a piece of paper. She stepped to a door, made a stab at her hair and went in. She was back in a moment. Without looking at me she sat down and resumed her work.

I had hardly picked up a magazine when the same door opened and a middle-aged couple came out. It seemed to me that they left the office reluctantly and that they were annoyed. The phone rang. The receptionist answered and told me with a bewildered expression that I should go right in, Mr. Spencer was anxious to see me.

He was a slim, middle-sized man close to forty. He had dark-red hair, heavy brows, and precise brown eyes. He had a look of restless energy and restrained impatience.

He stood up behind the desk and I walked toward him across the big room with its wood paneling and shelves of legal tomes. He took my hand without smiling and said, "Well, where is she?"

"Barbara?" I sat down.

"Of course, Barbara."

"I don't know."

"You don't know?" He sank into his swivel chair and reached across the desk for a pack of cigarettes. "When did you see her last?"

"About four o'clock this morning."

"At her place?"

"No, mine."

He frowned at me across the flame of his lighter.

"She was with you until four? At your place?"

"More or less," I answered.

"Too vague," he said. "Which is it?"

"I'm not on the witness stand, Mr. Spencer," I said pleasantly.

His face colored. He got up and crossed to a window. For a moment he stared below in silence. He turned.

"Sorry, Elliot. The police just called. They're looking for Barbara. They have an APB out for her."

"Oh?"

"Yes, they want her on a murder charge. A new one. They figured I might know where she is. And I thought perhaps you came with news of her."

"What new murder charge?" I said.

He came back and sat down, leaning with an elbow on the desk, rubbing his brow.

"Vandiver," he said. "Shot and killed sometime last night at Barbara's house. Police got an anonymous call just a while ago. They believe Barbara did it."

I gave him a surprised face and made the appropriate sounds of astonishment. Then I said, "Do you think Barbara killed Vandiver?"

"Oh, my God, I don't know. I don't know what to think about Barbara any more. Does it matter? The police are convinced. And when they find her, I'm helpless. Completely. Money and legal maneuvers will do nothing for her. They'll hold her without bail."

"They can't hold what they haven't got," I said. "And I have a hunch Barbara won't be found easily. Besides, I don't think she killed Vandiver or anyone else."

He looked up at me with a wry smile and there was a hint of malice in his eyes. "Well, of course you're in love with her, aren't you, Elliot?"

"Well sure, aren't we all? Aren't you?" It was a meaningless remark said in anger, but not without a small intuition.

"What kind of a goddam question is that?" he shouted.

"Exactly the same sort you asked me."

"I'm a married man, you must know that!"

"Married men are invulnerable, is that it?"

I hoped he would go on protesting too much. But he glared at me a moment and then changed the subject.

"What is it you want from me, Elliot? I'm very busy."

"Barbara left me a note. And some money. A lot of money. She wants this thing cleared up before she comes out of hiding. And she made me a kind of agent to use the money as leverage. She's offering fifty thousand dollars reward to anyone among her circle of so-called friends and relatives who can give information leading to the arrest and conviction of the murderer of her parents."

"Fifty thousand," mused Spencer. "That *is* a lot of money. And you have the cash in your possession?"

"Yes."

"To disburse on your own judgment?"

"Absolutely."

"It's not a public, a general offer?"

"No."

"Well, I'll tell you, Elliot. In my opinion the idea is foolish, ridiculous. Assuming that Barbara is innocent, the only person in her circle who could give information about the murder of her parents is logically the murderer."

"Not necessarily," I said. "There are certain types who will keep their mouths shut in troublesome situations. They don't want to get involved. Until there's a strong smell of money. Then suddenly they remember a lot of things. Things they saw and heard, persons with hidden motives. In that way, secrets are aired. One guy sells out another—for money. Links begin to join links and finally there's a chain tied around someone's neck."

He nodded. "Perhaps."

"Besides, Barbara has nothing to lose. Cash on delivery. No conviction, no money. Oh, sure, it's a rather melodramatic approach. But not a foolish one at all."

"The money should be offered to the public via the newspapers," Spencer said. "The killing of Phyllis and Harvey Erickson has a professional cleverness to it. Possibly some hood was hired to do the job. And hoodlums will inform on hoodlums. For fifty thousand."

"True," I said. "But some of the neatest bombs have been made by amateurs with technical skill they got from a hobby or sideline. Barbara thinks this is a family affair, so to speak. Someone connected directly or indirectly with the Ericksons. Her guess should be better than most. She may have reasons she's not revealing. The newspaper bit, the professional angle, can be exploited later."

Spencer spread his hands in a gesture of resignation.

"So what do you want from me, Elliot? I'm still just as busy as I was ten minutes ago."

"I want fifty thousand dollars worth of information. I want you to head me in the right direction."

He leaned forward across the desk. "Listen, I could use fifty thousand. I could use ten—nicely. But if I could have made so much as an educated guess, I would have taken it to the police a long time ago."

I handed him the list Barbara had given me. He studied it, frowning.

"Most of these people benefited from the will in one degree or another," he said. "Barbara most, of course. She was the favorite. But I don't think it was purely a crime for gain. I believe it was a crime of passion. Jealousy, hatred, revenge. I would look into Harvey Erickson's background. He was a skirt-chaser, Class A. He was also a cold-blooded sonofabitch. He had a big smile and a big pocketbook. Until he got what he wanted. Then he had no further use for the person who gave it to him. He was bored. He was finished. Men or dames, business or play, he was the same. With Harvey you had to hold back a little, turn your aces up one at a time, striptease him along. Understand?"

"Sure. What about his wife, this Phyllis? Who hated her?"

"I don't know. That's a tough one. A beautiful woman, Phyllis was. Not a bad sort at all. I don't see a motive for her death. Another woman who hated them both, maybe."

"Where would you start with that list?"

He lighted a cigarette, picked up the paper, scratching his ear.

"Well, if you're going to use money as the wedge, skip over people who have plenty of it for the time being. Don't bribe the chef with a banquet, understand? So that cuts out the brother, Charlie Erickson. He came in second behind Barbara for a slice of Harvey. Didn't need it much anyway because he's a pretty big citrus grower, acres and acres of oranges, you know.

"Then there's the partner, Don Huffman, a bookkeeper at heart, plodded into a good thing. Mild and incapable of all this sinister intrigue. Also rich. Talk to him last.

"And let's see here… Pass over the stepsister, Lois Erickson or Lois Imhoff, that's her married name. Jesus, there's one you wouldn't miss in Grand Central at the rush hour. But pass over her because she lives in New York, was there when it happened. As for the others, toss them into a hat and pick one. Any one."

"There must be a best bet in light of what you know," I said.

He cocked a finger and snapped the list. "Well, all right. Try this one. Enid McKnight. She was Harvey's number one hobby for a long time. He got bored with her finally and went back to playing the field. But for a while I thought she might even replace Phyllis. When you meet her you'll see why. She must be hocking the jewels and furs by now. She didn't get honorable mention in the will. Though she deserved it. She had a special talent to hold Harvey so long. Understand? Try her."

Spencer walked with me to the door.

"Sure you won't tell me where to find Barbara?" he asked. "That girl is in a lot of trouble and she needs help."

"If I knew where she was, I'd go to her myself," I said.

He nodded. "I see. Well, good luck then, Elliot. And if you

have any more questions, call me."

CHAPTER 8

Enid McKnight wasn't home. I called her number the minute I left Spencer's office. Then I drove to my place with the intention of ringing her again from there.

I looked eagerly in my mailbox. I had a peculiar loss of time sense. So many events telescoped, all of them alien to my way of life, gave the illusion that Barbara had been gone long enough to write. Of course there was nothing from her. Two bills and a post card from one of my students vacationing in Catalina.

It was going on six o'clock. There was a steak in the refrigerator. I broiled it, heated some canned vegetables and ate without relish or appetite. I was cleaning up the dishes when the phone rang.

I dashed for it, barked hello repeatedly without getting a response. Someone on the other end had gone with my first words. I slammed the receiver down. Ordinarily, that would have been my only reaction. But now every little foreign episode had a sullen meaning, was a threat.

For a moment I sat at my desk speculating, building trouble for myself. I reached for the phone book. I had forgotten Enid McKnight's number. Absently I opened the book and began to thumb pages when something caught my eye and I stopped. In the D section there was a pen line under one of the names. I don't use green ink and I seldom mark my phone books or I might not have given it a second thought. I checked the name and got a surprise then I read:

DIETRICH CHARTER SERV
chartrd airplns

Barbara's letter to me was in green ink and I was positive that Mr. Dietrich and company could tell me where she had gone.

I called the Detrich Charter Service in high excitement. But the man who answered said he had just returned from flying someone to a ranch in North Dakota and he did not know if anyone by the name of Barbara Erickson had chartered a plane. He suggested that I get in touch with Earl Dietrich, who was at home. He gave me the phone number.

Dietrich answered and I didn't know quite how to begin because it had occurred to me that he might consider the information confidential. I decided it might be best to talk to him in person and told him so.

"Listen, fella," he said. "If you want to fly out of the country without papers, something like that, forget it. We work a strictly regulation taxi service and we don't deviate for a yard of clams under the table."

"Right," I said. "But I'm not even leaving the city, let alone the country. I'd like to talk to you on a personal matter. It concerns a very close friend of mine—Barbara Erickson."

There was an interval of silence more revealing than speech.

"What's your business, Mr. Elliot? Is this a legal matter?"

"Not at all. I'm a teacher. Barbara was in a class of mine."

"All right," he said. "You come over here prepared to prove it." He gave me an address in nearby Westwood and hung up.

It was dusk by now, and, as I was leaving, I reached for a lamp near a window on the street side. It was my habit to leave one light burning when I went out for the evening. But as my fingers groped for the switch, I happened to look towards the street and changed my mind.

Two men, bulky, but otherwise indistinguishable in the gloom, were coming down the walk. They moved with the light quick steps of purpose, yet darted furtive glances to the windows of the building, as if orienting themselves in an unfamiliar setting.

How did I know they were coming to my door? I didn't. But every instinct told me that they would connect with Barbara and that they were trouble.

I stood there in the semidarkness, waiting. I remembered the gun, but it was in the glove compartment. I heard some shuffling in the hallway and the murmur of low voices. Then the bell rang. I moved on tiptoe to the door and held myself, rooted, listening against the panel.

A foot scraped, the bell rang again.

"I know the bastard's in there," mumbled a heavy voice.

"Sure," said the other. "He was there just now when we called. You stay here. I'll hop around back, case he sneaks out that way."

But I was faster and he didn't know the building. I danced across the rug and got out the kitchen door without being seen. I drove to the corner where there was a phone booth outside a grocery store. I called the police and told them to send a squad car to the apartment house. I said I was just passing the building and saw two men who looked like they were trying to break into one of the apartments. I hung up.

Whoever they were, that would take care of them. For a while. But my God, how the tension was growing in me! Two days ago I was a fairly average guy in pretty ordinary circumstances. Since then I had been, however objectively, involved in two murders. I had been shot at, ambushed in my back yard, and now I was being hunted by characters unknown and determined. Even if I wanted to say, "Barbara, it's too deep and deadly for me, let's call the whole thing off," I was probably much too late. Besides, how did I find Barbara?

I hurried over to Dietrich's address to see if he had the answer.

CHAPTER 9

Earl Dietrich came to the door at my ring. He lived on the sixth floor of a large apartment building west of the main drag. He told me later that he lived alone; he had been divorced for several years.

He was a tall man and very blond, with a freckled skin flushed red from the sun. He looked close to forty, had a big muscular frame, solemn green eyes and an air of casual assurance. He wore light gray Daks and a dark gray sport shirt.

"Ross Elliot?" he said.

"That's right."

He stuck out his hand and smiled cautiously. I judged him to be a type who had few insecurities and wasted little charm on strangers.

I entered a large living room of soft-white walls surrounding deep sofas and chairs of pastel greens and blues, harmonic and restful blends of color. There were two enormous matching table lamps in black with white shades, an electric organ of blond mahogany, and a fieldstone fireplace overhung with a marvelously turbulent seascape.

Dietrich nodded to a chair. He leaned back against the mantelpiece, toyed with the prop of a model plane, waited for me to speak.

"I'm trying to locate Barbara Erickson," I opened. "She wrote me a letter asking me to attend to some personal interests of hers. I want to help but I need more information. There are details I should discuss with her. But now I can't find her. She's just disappeared."

Dietrich gave the prop a final flick with his finger, set the plane back on the mantel and folded his arms.

"Well, of course," he said, "I don't know any more than

you've told me, but it seems to me that if she wanted people to find her, she'd have announced where she was going." He smiled coolly.

"That's true," I said. "But Barbara went off in a state of confusion. She wasn't thinking too clearly."

Again he smiled. "If you're from the police, why don't you say so, Mr. Elliot?"

"I have nothing to do with the police."

"Private detective?"

I had brought along my teaching certificate and other identification. I handed them over. He studied and returned them.

"Not that I wouldn't cooperate with the police," he said. "But Barbara, loosely speaking, is a friend. And I think the police have been hounding her unnecessarily. Harvey Erickson had his own plane, you know. But he was a lousy flier. If he had to navigate farther than Burbank in a cloudless sky, he was in trouble. So I used to pilot him on cross-country hops. Maybe he wouldn't use me more than half a dozen times a year. But if he called in the middle of the night, I would be ready to shove in an hour. Because on the first of every January, he gave me a check for ten thousand clams."

"Mighty generous," I said.

"Not really. He took it off his income tax. Business, he called it. Huh! Two-legged business. A doll would meet him at every airport: That was his business. And he gave it to them—the business. No, he had the loot and he spent it when it pleased him. But he was one very demanding sonofabitch."

"And Phyllis Erickson? What sort was she?"

"All right, I guess. Though I didn't like her much either. A cute trick but a real digger. No blue in the blood, no polish, but she thought Erickson's money bought her a pedigree and a throne. Treated me like a chauffeur when she spoke at all. Maybe that's why I didn't like her."

"What about Barbara?"

"Now you're talking." He lit a cigarette and sat down on the arm of a chair. "A sweet kid, and sharp. My favorite. Though, to tell you the truth, I don't know her much better than I knew Harvey or Phyllis Erickson. Like I said, I was just an airborne chauffeur and the pay was great."

"All right," I said. "Assuming that you were willing to trust me, could you tell me where to find Barbara?"

"Nope."

"You couldn't?"

"Nope."

"Strange. Because she was at my apartment last night, and after she had gone I happened to be looking for a number in the phone book. And I came across your name. She had underlined it in that green ink she uses. So naturally, I thought—"

"And you were right," he interrupted. "She did phone me. She asked me if I would fly her to Acapulco and also keep my mouth shut. I said I would—both. That was early this morning. She was supposed to be out to the field at ten. She never showed up and she never called. I haven't heard from her since."

"Oh, Christ," I moaned. "That doesn't sound good."

"You got a big thing for her, haven't you?" he said with the first really warm smile. "I can see the arrow sticking clear through your ribs."

That was when he made me a drink and I opened up and told him the whole story. He was a pretty decent guy once he understood I was in Barbara's camp. But I let him wait to find out about Vandiver in the morning papers.

"Well," he said. "You'll hear from Barbara sooner or later. Meantime, you take that fifty thousand and hang it on a string and some of those monkeys will reach for the long green bananas. They'll talk like politicians at a convention."

"You have absolute faith in Barbara? You don't believe that she—"

"Never. She's incapable. Don't give it a thought."

"You were on the inside," I said. "You must have heard something. Got any ideas?"

He shook his head. "No, I've thought about it a lot. Could be any one of those people on that list Barbara gave you. Or none of them. Bomb like that has a professional stink to it. Bombs and silencers, both used by the pros. If not a pro, maybe someone with a pro background. You read about a case like this and nine times out of ten when they trace the guy down he's no beginner. He's got a history. Maybe he tried something like it before. Maybe he went to jail—way back. If I were you, I'd take every one of those names and get someone in the police department to search their backgrounds, see what other trouble they might have been in."

It was a damn good idea and I told him so. At the door he said to shout if I needed help. Meanwhile, if Barbara called he would have her get in touch.

I left feeling better, not so much alone. I rang Enid McKnight from a drugstore and she was home. At the very mention of money for information, she told me to come right over. "And bring a fifth of bourbon please, Mr. Elliot. A horde of parasites descended upon me last night and the place is drier than a WCTU picnic. Do hurry!"

CHAPTER 10

When I saw Enid McKnight's place in Glendale, I had some doubts about that party in which a "horde of parasites" consumed her liquor. It was a tiny guest cottage in back of a shabby house. Three would have been a crowd and six a jam. The furnishings were fire-sale modern, and if there had been any bottles of her own at the party, they were the kind she would take back for the deposit.

Enid herself was another matter entirely. She made a liar out of her surroundings. She was tall. In her late twenties. She had chestnut hair that tumbled far down the sweet concavity of her back. She had a great red bloom of mouth in a sensual heart of a face. Her smile was a small white challenge and her figure invited nothing less than awesome contemplation.

When she opened the door I handed her the bourbon and silently offered a posthumous hymn of praise to Harvey Erickson. This, though I was certain that Enid McKnight would be an intellectual midget. I was quite wrong.

"Come in," she said, taking the bottle in its sack as if it were the nectar of life and holding it lovingly aloft. "And thank you for this."

"I never thought to ask if you needed some mix."

She closed the door. "With this? Oh, no. Unless it's Old Harvest Moon or something equally corrosive, I drink it cozy with just a *pffft* of ice." Her lips pursed charmingly, she cradled the bottle in an area well suited for cradling. "Sit down, Mr. Elliot and don't let this place frighten you. I call it Hangover Inn. I had a horrible dream one night and when I awoke in the morning I looked around and, my God, it was reall Shall I fix yours cozy, too?"

"Please. With just a *pffft* of ice."

She smiled, departed in a whisper of long limbs, disappeared.

During the first few minutes after she returned with the drinks, I gave her a capsule biography. In turn, she told me that she had once been assistant to the manager of a travel bureau in New York, and there she had met Harvey Erickson. She admitted quite frankly that there had been an affair, and that Erickson had brought her to the coast with the alleged intention of marrying her as soon as he could arrange a divorce and settlement with his wife. She believed that he was quite serious. At the time.

These introductions over, she abruptly set down her glass, entwined her fingers and gave me a long appraising look. I noticed that under the stronger light in which she sat, her face showed signs of dissipation and stress. Her eyes were puffy and underlined with shadowy half-moons; in repose there were tiny inroads of fatigue at the corners of her mouth.

"Now," she said. "You need information and"—she looked around her—"obviously I need money. Let's begin."

"Well, I wish it were that simple… Enid? Do you mind?"

She shook her head. "I hate formality."

"You see, Enid, as I told you on the phone, I have a large sum of money for anyone who can give me information leading to the murderer of Harvey and Phyllis Erickson. But it has to be precise information. It has to be more than gossip. It has to result in an arrest and conviction. No conviction, no money. Those are the terms."

"How much, Ross? How much money?"

"Fifty thousand."

"Fifty thousand! God—my own mother isn't safe. Whose money? Certainly not yours. Is it?"

I had to smile. "No, but thanks. It belongs to Barbara Erickson. She's making the offer."

She looked at me with some astonishment.

"Barbara! Not really!"

"Really."

"Of all people. You're a good friend of hers?"

"You might say that."

"Well, I'm sorry," she said, "but I never could quite believe in her innocence. Excuse me, but I need another drink."

She came back from the kitchen with the bottle and a bowl of ice. She poured generously for us both.

"Do you know Barbara well?" I asked.

"I only met her once. She was polite, but frigid. I suppose she hates me—because of her father. She knew, of course." Enid crossed her legs and drank hungrily. "But from the newspaper accounts anyway, it seemed to me that she had both opportunity and motive. And then there was the anniversary card in her handwriting."

"I know all that, Enid. The newspapers imply and expand. It sells papers. I'm on Barbara's side. And I don't think she'd pay fifty thousand for her own conviction. So let's assume she's innocent and take a look at the others." I passed her Barbara's list and she studied it with squinting interest.

"Well, then, let's go to New York first," she said.

"Oh?"

"Oh, yes. For some very dirty dirt. And in New York we find Lois Imhoff. That's her married name. But she's Barbara's stepsister. From Phyllis' first marriage. Frank Imhoff, her husband, is manager of a wholesale hardware company. But that's unimportant.

"Before she got married, Lois lived with the Ericksons. She's about, oh…twenty-three, I guess. But when she was eighteen, something happened in the good old Erickson homestead. Harvey got drunk one night. Phyllis was at a bridge party and Harvey and Lois were alone. Harvey walked into her bedroom and found her *au naturel*—you know? And then the chase began. Harvey caught her and he—he raped her."

"My God!"

"Yes, and she became pregnant. From the very first she

wanted to go to the police with the whole thing, but Phyllis talked her out of it. Instead she was flown to Cuba, where she had an abortion. And from there to New York, where she remained until she was married. I think the money Harvey left her was conscience money. But she hated him. Oh, how she hated him! So try Lois for motive."

"How did you find this out?"

"From an unimpeachable source, as they say. But I promised not to divulge same." Enid poured herself a generous drink and sighed.

"Don't forget that Phyllis was also killed," I said. "And that she was Lois' mother."

"I'm not forgetting. There was no love lost between those two either. And the way the will was established, most of the estate went to Phyllis, with the others getting damn little unless she died first. So she would have to be gotten out of the way. At the same time? How neat!"

"Lois was in New York when it happened," I said.

"Did you ever hear of long-distance arrangements for a funeral, darling? With others handling the sordid details? If you're going to really dig, nothing can be overlooked."

"True," I said. "And you're a fountain of information. Anyone else on the list?"

She squinted once more at the names. "I know nothing about this Vandiver and very little about the partner or the brother, Barbara's uncle. I've never heard anything off key concerning them. No, I guess that's all I can tell you."

She got up and, swaying slightly brought the paper to me. I tucked it in my pocket.

She stared down at me with those big eyes narrowed, a silly grin on her face. "You won't forget where you got the word, will you, sweetie? It's the first time I ever told anyone. Honest. Do you think it might be worth fifty thousand?"

"Maybe."

She chuckled. "Fifty thousand. Fifty, fifty, fifty… God, how

I could use it!"

"Guess I'd better go," I said.

"Oh, no, no, no," she said. "Don't go. Please don't go. I'm so blue. I just can't tell you how blue I am." Her eyes clouded and I thought she was going to cry. Suddenly she sank to my lap and put her arms around me.

For a moment I did nothing. I just sat there, surprised and ineffectual. Then, slowly, I put my arms around her and she trembled against me. To tell the truth, I didn't even think of Barbara. Or fidelity, True Love, and the rest of those soap-opera platitudes. If I thought anything, it was that this was one very delicious hunk of woman and I wanted her.

She turned her head, the moist blossom of her mouth parted and melted over mine. A hand caressed my shoulder, wound up the nape of my neck. Soft fingers toyed with the lobe of an ear while her tongue stabbed and curled within the kiss.

I worked at the buttons of her jacket. But she pushed away, got unsteadily to her feet. With a small careful smile, she crossed the room to a record player. Music throbbed from it in a slow beat.

"Let's dance," she said, removing the jacket, draping it over the one lighted lamp so that the room was all but dark.

I got up and walked toward her. She was unzipping the skirt, pulling it off. She wore no slip or bra and suddenly, but for white lace panties, she stood naked. Her great pink-white breasts rose in impudent swells, dark centered, demanding.

"You're tight," I said.

She pulled me against her, undoing my coat, wrenching at my tie, unbuttoning my shirt. "I want to dance with you," she murmured. "Like this. In the nude."

We embraced around the room in a trance. And then across the floor and into her bedroom. But even as the music died and we fell together upon her bed, the phone rang.

"My God," she sighed. "What horrible timing." She threw on a robe. "Only a moment, darling," she whispered, and floated away, pulling the door to without closing it.

I heard snatches. At first she sounded puzzled. "Yes, it is.... I know, but why do you... Yes, he is but I don't see... Are you sure?... I can't believe it, you must be mistaken." And then, urgent and distressed, intensely sober. "Well, I don't know if I can.... Yes, but I dont' want to, I don't want to!... No, I just can't be involved.... Well, yes, I realize... No, I wouldn't want you to do that.... All right, I'll try. When will you... I see... Yes, I promise. Good-bye."

She came back, let the robe fall. For a moment she stood uncertainly in shadow. I could see only the stark beauty of her outline. But tension surrounded her.

"What's the matter?" I said. "Who was that?"

She sank to the bed and settled against me. "Just a pest who wanted to come over, darling. I had to promise to see him to-morrow to get rid of him. Shall we forget him?"

She kissed me hungrily but her body was rigid and her lips trembled. We made love as strangers committed to a calculated intimacy. The mood, the flavor of abandonment, had gone. Her touch seened mechanical. Her mind was absent, frenzied with trouble.

After a while I got up and began to hunt for my clothes.

"Where are you going? Ross, where are you going?"

"Home."

"Why?"

"It's late," I said. But knew it was because she was afraid and the fear had communicated.

"Don't go. Please!"

"Sorry. Maybe some other time."

"Do you want me to be lonely? I'll be so lonely now."

She said it without conviction and I didn't answer. I dressed rapidly. I had an urge to hurry, to run out of the place. I saw that she was dressing also, in a blouse and skirt. She went with me to the door. Her expression was odd. She stood frozen, almost as if listening.

I took her by the shoulders and made her look at me.

"Tell me," I said.

"Tell you what?"

"Who called and why you're afraid." I shook her. "Goddam it, tell me!"

"I can't," she said. "Please go now."

I gave her one last searching glance; then, on intuition, hearing her steps behind me, I crossed to the kitchen and went quickly out the back door.

CHAPTER 11

I saw him the moment I closed the door. The huge shadow of him stepped from behind a tree and sprang toward me, gun in hand. I fell easily and rolled in a ball at his oncoming feet. When he went down across me, I shoved up and sent him over on his back. He was in a sitting position and the gun barrel was lifting when I kicked the side of his head like a football. He fell sideways without a sound, and I had his gun in my hand when I saw the other one loping up behind me, pausing, taking aim.

He fired, missed. I fired back wildly and ran around the behind a bush. When he had gone, I raced softly for my car.

I got moving before he caught on. There was no shot but I saw lights flare and burst after me. I made a right and then another. In the middle of the next block I saw a dark apartment house with a private lot. A good dozen cars were packed tightly but I spied a single open space in the glare of my lights. I braked and swerved, cut in between two cars and hit the light switch with my palm as I cut the motor. He rounded the corner and slammed on by in an angry whine of sound.

I slumped in my seat and didn't stir for nearly an hour. Then I backed in darkness and drove to within a block of Enid's house. On foot I sneaked to a position across the street and watched a long time. The cottage was dark and there seemed to be no one about. I circled and crept into the back yard. I waited, staring from behind a tree. Then I tiptoed around to the side and found an open window. I made a small hole in the screen and released the latch with my finger. I hoisted myself into the living room without a sound.

I stood in her bedroom doorway, adjusting to the darkness. She lay on her back. A sheet covered her to the waist. Her long hair spilled around her in disorder. I approached her bed on the balls of my feet.

Suddenly she sat up, I should have known she would not be able to sleep. Immobile as a statue, she stared in my direction. I leaped forward and clamped a hand over her mouth. She struggled in a frenzy of fear.

"Stop it!" I barked in a hoarse whisper. "It's Ross Elliot." She subsided but I twisted her arm behind her before I took my hand away.

"Ross," she said. "Please!"

"Quiet! Speak softly."

"Ross, I thought you… You're hurting my arm—please! What do you want?"

"Who were those men?"

"I—I don't know. I heard shots and I—"

"Come on, Enid. I'm not playing!" I twisted her arm tighter. "Who were they?"

"The police."

"What!"

"Yes, honest. The police." In the gloom, touched by moonlight from the window, her white face was upturned beseechingly, her naked breasts heaved and shimmered.

"You're lying!" I said.

"No. Someone must have told them you were here. They called and asked me to keep you from leaving. I didn't want to, but they said if I didn't they'd hold me in jail for questioning. After you left, about ten minutes later, they were back. They gave me their names and a police number to call if you got in touch with me."

"All right," I said, releasing her arm. "Why?"

"Larry Vandiver is dead. He was murdered. At Barbara's house. You're under suspicion because you were seen leaving her house after it happened. Someone got your license number. They're looking for both you and Barbara. Especially Barbara, I gathered. And that's all I know."

"I'm sorry if I hurt you," I said. "The whole thing had a different kind of smell. Now listen, Enie. I didn't kill Vandiver. Barbara didn't kill Vandiver. But I'm going to find out who did, among other things. And you haven't seen or heard from me, understand?"

"I don't know about Barbara," she said. "But I don't think you would kill anyone, Ross. I won't call the police."

I leaned down and gave her a quick kiss. She clung to me. There was about her a faintly repulsive odor of raw bourbon. I unfastened her arms gently. Then I left her. I went out by the back door and drove home without being followed.

There was no one lurking about my apartment. I made sure before I went in. I was now quite positive that the two men who had come to my place earlier were detectives and the same ones. It amused me, though not very much to think that I had called the police to get rid of them.

I blacked out the bedroom windows and quickly packed a suitcase. This, after I sat by the phone for several minutes trying to decide if I should turn myself in. It seemed to me that, especially after the fracas on Enid's lawn, once in jail I would be a long time getting out. Meanwhile, I would be as useless to Barbara as to myself.

Just before I closed the suitcase, I reached in my pocket and found the gun I had taken from the detective. It was a .38 revolver, police special. I couldn't think what to do with it. Mail it? To whom? Drop it at the nearest precinct? Ha! I tossed it into the suitcase, snapped the lock and got out of there in a hurry.

An hour later, under the name Arthur C. Baldwin, I was checked in at the Biltmore, in the heart of L.A. I was lying on the bed, smoking and leafing through the classified section of the phone book under Detective Agencies. Finally I came across the familiar name of a national branch. I wrote down the number, closed the book and turned out the light. I was too exhausted to feel fear or anything at all.

I fell asleep immediately.

CHAPTER 12

Vandiver's murder was front-page news the next morning. Barbara was being hunted the country over. Because of her wealth and her unproven connection with the murder of her parents, there were columns of background on her. And a picture— a dim likeness which must have been taken years ago, for it was a happy college-girl face, sadly eager and immature.

To my vast relief, there was not a mention of me, though there were hints. It was believed that Barbara was not alone in the house at the time of Vandiver's murder and that a man whose identity "was not disclosed by the police" might have fled with her from the scene of the crime.

On the second page there was a picture of the house—and one of Van diver's shrouded body being carried from it as a solemn crowd watched with vacant faces.

The first thing I needed was cash, a great deal of it if I was to move around in secrecy, paying people to get things done, unable to chance more than one visit to the bank before it too was watched or alerted. Consequently I was among the first to enter when the doors opened that morning. I had to see Harry Burgess, one of the vice presidents, in order to get an okay on my check for five thousand. I had an uneasy moment when Burgess went off to another part of the bank with the check. But he was only investigating my balance and brought the money back with him, mostly in hundreds.

I took a taxi to the hotel. I had stopped using my car (it was stored in a garage) because the police would be looking for it.

I called the detective agency from my room. I declined their invitation to drop over to their office for a chat. Instead I spoke expansively of money for services and they had an operative knocking at my door in half an hour. We shook hands and I gave him my phony name. His card said he was Maurice Rumbaugh.

He was a graying, portly guy close to fifty, and not impressive physically. But he had eyes like steel filings, he seemed knowledgeable and willing. He was also a former FBI man, and that *was* impressive.

After he assured me that all matters were strictly confidential, whatever their nature, I told him that I was representing a member of the Erickson family, related to the late Harvey Erickson. I said that my party did not believe. Barbara Erickson was guilty of any crime, new or old, and wanted a check run on certain members of the family and their friends.

I had to hand it to Rumbaugh. He must have seen the furor in the morning papers and he must have been stirred by intense curiosity. But he kept a poker face and asked no questions. He simply said in his soft-voiced, almost funereal manner, that of course he would make every effort but it was a very large order if I wanted a thorough investigation.

I told him a thorough investigation might come later, but for the moment I wanted only a check to see if any of the people on the duplicate list I gave him had a criminal record or anything approaching the same. I said that a leisurely approach would not do at all, that I wanted the information fast and was willing to pay for speed and all the help he needed. To prove it, I gave him three hundred dollars as a retainer. He gave me a receipt and promised to phone me at four that afternoon.

I spent the day alternately reading and pacing. I had both grim and loving thoughts about Barbara. It depressed me to think that even now she might be calling me at my apartment. It never occurred to me to doubt her. At least if it did, I shoved the thought from my mind.

I had lunch in my room, I never left it. At two minutes after four the phone rang. It was Rumbaugh.

"Think I have something that might interest you, Mr. Baldwin," he said. As always, he spoke without excitement, his voice as flat and soporific as the chant of a train announcer.

"Fire away," I said.

"Well, sir, far as I can determine, none of these people on the list were even so much as in the drunk tank for a night."

"Oh?"

"Yes, sir, but one of the names struck a big gong in my head. Guy isn't even on the list but his wife is—this Lois Imhoff, married to Frank Imhoff. I once worked on a case involving a Frank Imhoff. That was a long time ago, but it came back to me. So I checked New York and it's the same character.

"Now this Imhoff has a record dating back to '34 when he was a very bad boy—car theft, assault with a deadly weapon, breaking and entering, armed robbery, *ad nauseum*. He did a stretch in Elmira, another in Sing Sing, and one in Leavenworth on a federal rap. They got nothing on him since. Not on paper, that is. But he was suspected of running a syndicate book with this wholesale hardware business as a cover. The investigation was hot and then it died altogether. Could have been a payoff. But on the record, Imhoff's been clean for years."

"Wow! Anything else?"

"Nope. Except that this hardware business has been running in the red and Imhoff has been living hard-up until recently when he bought a nice layout on Long Island and a new Cad."

"His wife inherited," I said. "That could explain it."

"Maybe. And one other item. It may have no connection, but I like it. A guy who worked for this hardware company, name of Pederson, got himself blown to hell one night about five years ago. Sound asleep when it happened, mind you. Bomb in a brief case under his bed. Three in the morning—wham! They never could trace down who did it or why."

"My God!"

"You want me to go on nosing around, Mr. Baldwin?"

I thought about that a moment. "No, just hold tight a while until you hear from me."

"You want me to mail the written report to your hotel?"

"No. Keep it there on file. I'll drop by soon and pick it up.

And thanks a lot. For a damn good job!"

I hung up and then called Earl Dietrich. He was out at the field in one of the hangers and it took them about five minutes to get him to the phone. He sounded breathy and a little put out. I told him I wanted to charter one of his planes. I asked him if he would personally fly me to New York and be ready in a couple of hours.

"I don't take many runs myself any more," he said. "I have a lot of paperwork here, administrative stuff. I have a good man for you though."

"Well, I realize that, Earl. But this has to do with the Erickson case and I'd like to kick around some ideas with you en route."

"Christ! Did you read the papers this morning?"

"Sure did. How about it? Will you go?"

"How long will you be in New York?"

"Couple of days maybe. I'll want you to wait and fly me back. I'll pay all expenses and a bonus for the layover on top of the charter fee."

After a silence he said, "Okay, it's a deal. I'll get a weather check and gas up one of the Bonanzas. See you in a couple of hours."

* * * *

Earl Dietrich hoisted my suitcase into the luggage compartment of the sleek blue-and-cream Beechcraft Bonanza. He sealed the compartment door, said, "Hop aboard, Ross, and let's get flying." He grinned. "Or we'll never make it before dark."

Tall and blond, heavy jawed and muscular, Dietrich looked handsome—almost the Hollywood version of the fighter pilot. He wore a tan business suit, no hat. For a ridiculous moment I found myself surprised and even disappointed that neither helmet nor goggles sat rakishly upon his head.

I climbed in and we fastened seat belts. The starter whined, the prop spun, the engine caught and held in a steady roar. He adjusted the radio and for a moment spoke to the control tower.

We taxied to a runway, swung into the wind and braked while the engine warmed. He spoke again to control, opened the throttle and hurled us into the dying afternoon, up, up, banking gently, making the turn, nosing on course.

For a time, as I confided in Dietrich about Frank Imhoff, L.A. sprawled endlessly below. The first lights winked somberly in the gathering dusk. Outlying towns and cities, like fluorescent grape clusters, faded behind. And night spread itself softly over the shadowy ghost of the desert.

Dietrich poured coffee from a thermos and passed me a cup. We sipped in silence for a minute. The engine droned with rhythmic assurance. Dietrich yawned. I was tense and excited.

"I'd like to bet," said Dietrich, blowing into his cup, "that Barbara Erickson is one scared little girl tonight. Wherever she is."

In the frail light of the instrument panel, I studied the line of his jaw. But didn't answer.

Again I was wondering who or what had prevented Barbara from showing up to take that flight to Acapulco.

CHAPTER 13

The following afternoon we landed at an airport on Long Island. I rented a car and we drove to Forest Hills where Lois and Frank Imhoff had a house on Greenway North in the Gardens section. During the flight Dietrich had loosened up and we had become quite friendly. He had offered to give me a hand if there was any trouble. Meanwhile he said he would work with me behind the scenes, we would talk over the situation as it developed and confer on a course of action—if any. I liked having Dietrich in my camp. He had been a jet pilot in Korea, he was smart and he was fearless.

We took a room together at the Forest Hills Inn, and that evening after dinner I drove over to the Imhoff place. In view of Frank Imhoff's reputation, I told Dietrich to check on me if I hadn't returned in a couple of hours. I gave him the address and phone number.

It was a sweltering night. My shirt was glued to my back by the time I braked in front of Imhoff's place—a two-story Tudor style house on a grassy corner lot, carefully landscaped. In such a neighborhood, the house would bring fifty thousand without an argument.

My thumb on the bell button brought a colored maid to the door. I gave her my name and told her I was a personal friend of Mrs. Imhoff's sister. She said she would take Mrs. Imhoff the message—Mr. Imhoff was not at home. This latter was no great disappointment to me.

The maid came back and walked me through a living room encumbered with French Provincial to a small study. On one wall of the study there was a head-and-shoulders oil of a young woman, apparently Lois Imhoff. I was studying it when she entered the room.

She was a slender blonde with one of those narrow fashion-plate figures which may be chic but, for me, only manage to seem boyish and sexless. Her features were the chiseled sort, smartly cut—from pure bone. She had biting gray eyes. But now she smiled and the face was suddenly young and not unpleasant.

"Mr. Elliot?"

"That's right."

"You're a friend of Barbara's?"

"I like to think so."

"Won't you sit down?"

She settled opposite me, her lips smiling, her eyes speculating and cautious.

"You're from California, Mr. Elliot?"

"Yes."

"Just visiting?"

"Not at all. I came expressly to see you."

"Me! Why, what on earth for?"

"Barbara sent me. She thinks you might have some clue as to who killed her father and your mother."

"Nonsense! If I knew anything, I would have told the police. My own mother! Has Barbara gone mad?"

"I don't think so. I have fifty thousand dollars she left with me to give anyone who can solve this thing."

"You're not serious!"

"Perfectly."

"Fifty thousand." She clamped the tip of her tongue between her teeth. "Where is Barbara now? I mean, you can tell me, because of course I'd never mention it to anyone. If she can't trust me, well…"

"I don't know where Barbara is. I wouldn't tell anyone if I did."

"She certainly is in a lot of trouble," sighed Lois. "Poor Barbara. No, not poor. That's an unfortunate word, isn't it?" She laughed dryly. "Sad is a better definition. So now they think she killed Vandiver too. Imagine! How absurd. Did you say fifty thousand dollars? A gift?"

"A reward. Barbara wants desperately to prove her own innocence. The money is payable to anyone who can give some information that will solve those murders and convict the killer. I'm sure if you search your memory, Mrs. Imhoff, you can come up with some little clue. Anything. Even something you once considered unimportant or personal."

"Oh, I wish I could talk to Barbara. You have no idea where she is?"

"No idea. Well, how about it, Mrs. Imhoff?"

For a moment she was thoughtful. She frowned, chewed a nail. "How soon could I have the money?" she said.

"Just as soon as there's an arrest and conviction."

"Arrest and conviction. Conviction! Good God, that could take forever."

"Well, if there was enough evidence for an arrest, I'm sure we could work something out so that you could have a substantial advance payment. It all depends on how concrete the evidence is. In other words, if it seems obvious that on your information the police have taken the right person in custody, than I'm quite sure you wouldn't have to wait for a trial, just an indictment."

"I would need about ten thousand right away," she said quickly.

"That's possible. If there's an arrest. Do you really have something?"

She lighted a cigarette and her hand trembled. Her face had become contorted with fear. She made several false starts. She took a deep breath and shook her head. She smiled nervously.

"No," she said. "I'm afraid I don't have what you're looking for. No evidence at all. Just some wild guesses. I'm sorry. What you need is solid evidence and I don't have it."

"Even a wild guess can turn up evidence," I said excitedly. "Give it a try. Please?"

"No," she said firmly, "I'm sorry I brought it up. It was silly of me. You'd better go now, Mr. Elliot."

"Don't be afraid," I said. "You'll be protected. You were going to tell me about your husband, weren't you?"

Her jaw fell, her face blanched. "How did you know?" she said.

"I did some checking. Your husband has a record. So it stands to reason that—"

"Why does it stand to reason just because he has a record?"

"People tend to follow a pattern. Especially criminals. A few years of clean living don't necessarily wipe out the habits of a lifetime. Along comes a special opportunity and it begins again."

She sighed deeply. "I didn't know about his record when I married him, believe me. Still, it might not have made a bit of difference. But he lied to me and I found out about it secondhand. It doesn't matter now because I stopped loving him awhile back and became afraid of him. He's mixed up in something, I'm not sure exactly what. Some very odd men call here and Frank is gone for days at a time without telling me why. I want to leave him but I can't. He got control of the money I inherited and I don't have a dime of my own any more. We had a big scene about it and he made some horrible threats."

"There are laws, you know."

She laughed bitterly. "Not for Frank. He makes his own. And while it's not much of a life, I'd like to go on living. Life is like a bad play—confused, sordid, and pointless. But still you have this stupid compulsion to stay and see the end."

"Where is he now? Your husband, I mean."

"I don't know. I never really know. He didn't come home last night. It's been a long time since he even bothered to alibi his comings and goings. He has lots of intriguing little enterprises, I suppose. And other women. I hope he never comes back."

"And these wild guesses?"

"Just that—guesses."

"You think he planted that bomb, don't you?"

"I think, I think, I think!" She got up suddenly, crossed the room, turned. "And what good does it do to think?" She squeezed her brows between twitching fingers. A tear washed her cheek. "Oh, yes, maybe he did it. Or maybe he had someone do it for him. He was nearly broke before it happened. He needed money desperately to finance some scheme. He asked me if I could borrow from Harvey, my stepfather. And when I told him I wouldn't borrow from Harvey if I slept in Central Park and was dying of cold and starvation in mid-winter, he said, 'Why doesn't the sonofabitch die and leave you a bundle? Why doesn't he get hit by a truck? It could be arranged, you know.' That's just what he said."

"All right. Now, was he here in New York when it happened? And were you with him at the time?"

She fell into a chair and slumped towards me, twisting a handkerchief. "No," she said. "He wasn't here and I wasn't with him. He was supposed to be in Chicago. On business. Strangely, it was one of the few times he told me where he was going. He gave me the name of a hotel. But I didn't care and of course I didn't check."

"How soon after the bomb did he return?"

"Let's see...it was the following night. He pretended to be terribly sympathetic. Not about Harvey, because he knew I hated him, but about my mother. Yet just as soon as I calmed down a little, he started asking about the money, how much I would get."

"Anything else?"

"No. Except that he used my inheritance for some scheme that made him a big profit. And then he wouldn't return the money as he promised."

I wanted to leave then. But she kept needling me, asking me what her chances were of getting some quick cash for the information she had given me. Then she probed my connection with

Barbara and I had to satisfy her curiosity as quickly as possible. At last I was backing out of the room and she was following me to the front door.

"Did you have a hat?" she asked, opening a hall closet, peering up at a shelf containing half a dozen.

"We never wear them in California," I answered.

She was shutting the closet door when I saw something turquoise and familiar. I reached out and caught the door.

"What is it?" she asked.

"This," I said, taking the dress down from the rack, holding it up on its wire hanger. "Turquoise and wool knit. Beautiful. And unusual."

"Yes, well I'm glad you like it." She grabbed for it.

"It belongs to Barbara," I said. "She was wearing it only the other night. I'd know it anywhere."

"Oh," she said, her face changing swiftly from fearful surprise to a nervous simple-explanation smile. "Actually it's *my* suit. I loaned it to Barbara a long time ago and she just returned it. I sent it to the cleaners and I suppose the maid stuck it in here when it was delivered. How careless!"

"You're lying," I said.

"Now listen, how dare you come in here and—"

"When you have a million dollars," I interrupted, "you don't have to borrow someone else's clothes. And in the last few days, Barbara has been much too distracted to be mailing anything, even if she did borrow it. So that means that Barbara has been in this house. C'mon. Where is she!"

"I told you, Barbara sent me the—"

I grabbed her wrist and twisted.

"All right, all right," she cried. "Barbara was here. But she's gone and I don't know where."

"Why didn't you tell me?"

"Why should I? Maybe you're a policeman. How do I know who you really are?"

"You don't think I'm from the police. You believed me from

the beginning. Where's Barbara?"

"I don't know. Honestly. She rented a car and drove to Las Vegas. From there she got a plane to New York. She came out here and wanted me to hide her for a while. She didn't know about Frank—his background. I hadn't told her. Frank was at home and he never left us alone. He offered to hide her in a much safer place—with friends at Montauk Point. She agreed and I didn't dare protest. Frank drove off with her the next morning. When he got back he admitted he was lying, that he took her some place else. He said it was better if I didn't know where—the police could make me talk, but him, never."

"My God," I said. "How foolish, how dangerous."

"Yes, but I knew these people in Montauk Point and it would have been perfectly okay—if he had actually taken her there. Oh, I just can't think when Frank's around. He frightens me witless. But anyway, why should he want to harm Barbara?"

"I don't know," I said. "He may not want to harm her. And then again... I've got to find her!"

"How could you possibly find her now?" said Lois.

"That's one I'll have to think about. Meantime, forget that I was here. Forget that I have any connection with Barbara. You do want to help, don't you?"

"Of course. And if Frank turns out to be the one who..."

"Then you'll get the money. But try to find out where Barbara is and call me at the Forest Hills Inn."

"I will," she said. "Oh, God, if anything happens to Barbara..."

The thought gave me a sick hollow feeling. "In that case," I said, "something is going to happen to Frank Imhoff. Me!"

She called after me as I want down the walk. I didn't hear what she said but it had the breathy, frantic sound of a warning. I turned around, but she had closed the door.

I understood in the next moment. A blue Cadillac sedan turned into the driveway and braked sharply. There were three men in the car. I knew one of them must be Imhoff. I didn't want to confront him then. It was important to keep my identity and my purpose secret. I hurried to the rented Chevvy and was opening the door when I heard someone come up behind me. I swung to face him, certain it was Imhoff.

He was a chunky man with dark brows and dark complexion. He was neatly dressed in a suit that might have been blue Shantung. His hat was dark gray. The faint shine of sweat was on his arrogant face.

"Hey, buddy," he said. "Who're you?"

"Who wants to know?" I said lightly.

"Don't be smart, buddy. Just answer."

"My name is Buddy, you got it right. My friends call me Bud."

Behind him I saw that the other two had climbed from the Cadillac. They leaned against it, watching us. I turned to go but he caught my shoulder and heaved me around.

"Let me give you some advice," I said. "Take your goddam greasy paw off my shoulder!" I brushed the hand aside.

For seconds he stood coiled, motionless, indecisive. Then he smiled—a nothing smile.

"My name is Imhoff," he said. "You just came out of my house. When people come out of my house, I like to know who they are."

"Oh, well, that's different," I said. "I'm a salesman. The lady wasn't buying, so I left."

"What do you sell?"

"Magazines. All kinds. By subscription. Maybe you'd be interested. Now we have a three-year plan that—"

"Can it! You don't look the type for magazines. Show me identification."

"Are you a customer? I only show identification to customers." Once more I began to climb in and again he caught my shoulder. I came around fast and belted him in the mouth. He staggered, fell. I saw the other two racing toward me. Imhoff had come to his knees. In the light from the street lamp I saw the naked anger on his bloody face, the blackjack in his hand.

I couldn't seem to get the car started. There was the raw smell of too much gas. But I had the windows up and the doors locked before they reached me. Imhoff, on my side, was beating on the glass with the sap. A web of cracks appeared, a small hole in the center. The other two were drawing guns.

At that moment the car started and I plowed ahead. I saw them leap across the lawn for the Cadillac. But in a moment I had turned a corner. And then another.

They were too late.

CHAPTER 14

"From what you tell me," said Earl Dietrich, pacing our room at the Inn with a worried frown, "it's got to be Imhoff and his goons who planted that bomb. Even his own wife is convinced. So next we have to find Barbara. If she's still—"

"Don't say it!" I shouted. "Don't even think it!"

Dietrich chewed his lip, balled a fist which he beat into his palm. "Anyway," he said, "there's no logical reason for Imhoff to harm her. She's not a threat. She knows nothing about him, doesn't suspect him. No, with all the evidence against her, it would make more sense for him to tip the police, let them take her in for the rap."

"Who knows how a guy like Imhoff would think?" I said. "Guessing is a waste of time."

"Okay, you're right. We'll figure him later. First we find Barbara." Dietrich now sounded completely dedicated to the idea and I suddenly felt for him a strong liking and gratitude.

"What the hell can we do?" I asked. "Grab Imhoff and beat the truth out of him?"

"Not with two armed bodyguards," said Dietrich. "Best way is to park in sight of his house and keep a twenty-four-hour watch in shifts, eight hours apiece."

"And then follow him?"

"Right. But we'll need another car, and I've got a Ford convertible I rented while you were gone. I didn't want to sit around a couple of days without wheels of my own."

"Good enough. But why do we need another car?"

"Because Imhoff might recognize the one you were driving."

"True. So we'll trade cars and I'll take the first shift. You get some sleep, Earl."

"I'm about as sleepy as a tiger on the prowl for game," said Dietrich. "But I'll give it a try."

We exchanged car keys and I told Dietrich how to get to Imhoff's.

"I'll put in a call at the desk," he said. "I'll relieve you in eight hours. Meantime, if he goes out and you have to follow, give me a ring the first breather you get. But don't worry about it. If I don't see the Ford on the street, I'll know you're tailing him and I'll come back here to wait."

"Sure glad to have some help, Earl. I really appreciate it."

"Hell, I'd be bored goofing around," he said. "And Barbara needs finding. Fast! Now beat it before the bastard takes off and we lose him."

Dietrich was right. We almost did lose Imhoff. I hadn't been parked down the street from his place twenty minutes when the door opened and he came out, followed by his boys. They got in the Cadillac and came out of the drive in my direction. I slouched down until they had passed right by me; then I swung around and followed.

They were headed for some place farther out on the Island. Traffic was heavy and I had little trouble keeping cars between us. They drove hard on the speed limit but never above it. In a half-hour I was quite certain they were moving toward Long Beach. I was right.

We skirted around the city and took a shore road. Traffic thinned and I had to be more careful. The damp feel and briny smell of the ocean was in the air, but I could neither see nor hear it at the distance. We slid by clusters of houses on side streets which led to the beach.

At last the big taillights of the sedan brightened and winked off to the right, seaward. I didn't make the turn but waited at the corner, lights out, watching. It was a street of summer homes and cottages stretching to the beach. The Cadillac paused at the far end, swung into what must have been a driveway, disappeared.

I gave them five minutes and followed. The Cadillac was parked in the darkness beside a cottage fronting the ocean. A large overgrown lot separated the cottage from the nearest home. The cottage was dark. Absolutely. If there was light inside, none showed. I backed the Ford a half block away and returned on foot.

Cautiously, I moved out upon the beach before the cottage. Now the deep swirling sigh of the ocean was audible. A dark giant breathing—inhale to the sea, exhale to the shore. And again. And again. Endlessly.

I lay prone upon the beach under a clouding sky. The sand was still warm from the furnace of the day. I watched and waited. Twenty minutes, a half-hour. Then a car door slammed, footsteps approached along the beach, there was the glow of cigarettes. I heard two men talking, their silhouettes growing towards me. I had thought the slamming of the Cadillac door meant Imhoff was leaving. But now I understood that these were the guards who rode with him. They had been waiting outside in the darkness of the car all the time.

They were thirty feet away and coming on. Their voices had a hushed, secret sound. They spoke without clarity. Tensely, in terse phrases. I sprawled rigid, wishing I could burrow into the sand. Wind was washing a cloud from the face of the moon, and in another minute I would be revealed. I got ready to spring.

Then a door on the beach side of the house was cracked and a wisp of light arrowed the sand. There was a thin whistle—a signal sound. The figures turned, tossing butts and hurrying toward the car. Shortly I heard the muted throb of the motor. The car backed and turned. It sped away.

I sneaked over the beach to where the door had been cracked. It seemed possible that Imhoff had remained behind. I didn't see him leave and there was no telling. I found the door and, bending, saw a pale edge of light.

I stood listening. Hearing nothing, I was undecided. After a moment I knocked softly and ran around a corner of the house.

In seconds I heard a stealthy unlatching and someone appeared in the doorway. Just a shadow with an extended hand that must be holding a weapon. Then that cloud drifted from the moon and I saw the dull glint of steel. And recognized the person who held the tiny gun.

"Barbara," I whispered. "Barbara!"

She turned instantly and I held my breath. "Barbara," I said gently. "It's Ross. Ross Elliot." I stepped out.

She stood fixed in the moonlight. Then she danced toward me, took my hand without a word and pulled me inside.

In the darkness, I heard the door close and lock.

CHAPTER 15

For a moment she clung to me. We said nothing. I kissed her tremulous mouth. She made whimpering sounds. Then she was gone and a light glowed softly across the room.

She was dressed in a tan sweater and green skirt. Her strained face looked wan in the dark frame of her hair. Yet to me she was never so desirable. Even with the small automatic in her hand, aimed loosely in my direction.

"Is the gun for friends too?" I asked.

"Are you still a friend?" she said.

"And more," I answered.

"Of course, darling," she said. "And more. It was a stupid question. But I've been so nervous. And I thought you might have believed some of the things you read in the papers about me."

"Never," I said.

She set the gun on a table by the lamp. "Now I'm worried," she said. "If you could find me, so could the police. How in the world did you ever do it?"

"Just a lucky accident." I explained while she puffed incessantly on a cigarette, falling into a chair, rising to stand anxiously by the door, returning to sit in awkward and ever-changing positions.

"I guessed," she said, "that Frank made the best part of his living from some gambling racket. He dropped a few hints. And then, too, the characters he travels with are not exactly choir boys. But God, I never imagined for a minute that he might be behind these murders. I was even a little glad that he knew his way around on the other side of the law. He seemed so confident and capable about hiding me where I couldn't be found."

"You mean he actually told you that he's involved in some

racket?"

"Not exactly. But when I asked him about those tough looking men with him, he said they were a hangover from the old days when he used to have some gambling interests, and that one of the men owns the cottage and agreed to let me use it. He didn't fool me. I knew the old days were still here for him. And I didn't care a hoot about his gambling. He was very kind to me and he was doing me a big favor as far as I knew."

"Lois had never mentioned his background to you?"

"Never."

"Where did you get the gun?"

"He gave it to me."

"Crazy," I said. "Nothing adds up. Why did you come here? Why didn't you let Dietrich fly you to Acapulco as you planned?"

She looked at me with wide-eyed astonishment. "How did you know? Ross, how did you find out I was going to Mexico?"

I told her.

"I didn't know," she said irritably, "that you were spending all your time looking for me. I thought you wanted to help. I thought you would hire detectives and use the money to get evidence so that I could come home and be free and happy."

"Oh? Well, excuse me all to hell for sticking my neck out so far I nearly got it shot off." I walked to the door. "And meanwhile the police are looking for me all over the goddam country like an escaped convict. Excuse me, Barbara. I'll just leave before I louse you up any further."

I reached for the door but she came running across the room to me. She put her arms around me and held fast. She kissed my ear, her lips slid down my cheek and covered my mouth.

"Forgive me," she pleaded. "I'm tense and terribly frightened. And so ungrateful, darling. I didn't mean it."

We kissed eagerly and I told her that nothing short of this lovesick hunger for her could have involved me in her frenetic existence, though now it all seemed worthwhile and we might even be coming to the end of it. And the beginning of something else.

"Don't you care," she giggled, "that I'm so wealthy? I mean, won't you have all kinds of recriminations? Later?"

I laughed. "The dream ideal of Hollywood? Our hero loves her but scorns her money? Don't be silly. I'm delighted that you're rich. Maybe money can't buy happiness. Maybe. But how I love that green misery!"

We looked at each other and suddenly it wasn't funny. There wasn't a snicker left in the whole night. She went back to her chair and I said, "Now tell me why you didn't fly to Acapulco. Why did you make the arrangement with Dietrich and then not show up?"

"Simple," she said with a wave of dismissal. "I was too frightened. Earl is a nice guy, and under normal circumstances I would have trusted him to take me to the moon and keep it secret. But Earl Dietrich is also one of those steady, rule-book, right-is-right he-men. I was afraid he might turn me in at the last minute, so I decided against it. Then I thought of Lois. We've always been close and I knew she was the one person in the world, present company excepted, I could surely trust.

"I didn't dare fly a commercial airline out of L.A. So I rented a car and drove to Vegas. Then I took a plane which made connections to New York. Naturally, I didn't use my own name."

"Okay, that's clear enough. And finally," I said, crossing the room to stand over her and look her right in the eye, "did you kill Vandiver?"

She flinched, studied her cigarette, looked up at me. "No," she said. "I didn't kill Larry. But I knew you'd think I did."

"I had to fight back some doubts. But if you didn't kill him, who did?"

"I don't know. But I was there when it happened."

"What! You were there and you don't know?"

"It was dark and I couldn't see."

"Oh, my God. Then tell me from the beginning."

"It's complicated," she said. "And not very believable."

"Just tell me."

"Well, after you left that night, just after, I heard some queer sounds—a soft kind of popping. Twice."

"Shots," I said. "Fired at me with a silencer."

She nodded. "But I didn't know what it was then. It just made me uneasy. I put the light out quickly and climbed upstairs in the dark. I went to my room, which faces toward the Tillman place next door. The Tillmans were away. In the late spring they go to Cape Cod and don't return until fall.

"Well, I sat in a chair by the window listening for another of those sounds. Grizz was tied up in the kitchen by the back door. He hadn't even growled.

"Then I became aware of something wrong, misplaced. Nothing to do with those sounds, a visual thing. I was looking right at it, but for a few seconds I didn't get it. There was a dim light on behind the shade of a second-story window over at the Tillmans'. On the street side. It dawned on me slowly, the strangeness of that light, with the Tillmans away.

"Then the light went out and a man appeared at the front of the house, on the walk. He paused for just a second under a lamp, peering down the street and looking wild. Oh, just wild! I saw that it was Larry and I was sure that he had just come from that room and that he must hide there nights, watching me. He knew the place was empty—I had mentioned it. And he must have broken in at some time or other."

"So *he* shot at me after all," I said.

"I think so," she answered gravely. "I don't believe he intended to kill you, just scare you. Anyhow, in a moment he began to run down the street. Frantically. He disappeared around a corner and didn't come back."

"Sure," I said. "That was when he bolted for his car and slammed over to my place to wait for me. I was driving slowly, on top of which I was so goddam nervous I made a wrong turn. So he beat me there easily. Just before I tangled with him I saw butts on the ground by the glider and figured he had been there for quite awhile. But it must have been one of the tenants who couldn't sleep in the heat and went out for a smoke."

"Don't you want me to tell the rest of it, Ross?"

"Of course. I'm just getting oriented."

"She lighted a cigarette and I sat down on the arm of her chair. "I need a drink," she said.

"Better not."

"Why?"

"Because there isn't time to get sociable and cozy," I said. "Not here, anyway. I'll explain later. But now go on."

"Well, after Larry left I didn't know what to do. I thought of calling the police, but since he was gone it didn't make sense. And anyway, the last thing I needed was to get still more involved with the law. So instead I went across to the Tillmans' and tried the front door. It was locked. I had a flashlight and went around back. That door was open. Unlocked, I mean.

"I was scared to death but determined. I walked into that dark house and lighted my way to the stairs with the flash. I went up. It was the left front bedroom and I had no trouble finding it. The shades were drawn, the room was messy. The bed was rumpled, cigarette butts in a tray, half a sandwich on a table. There was also a dirty glass and a pint of whiskey, nearly empty.

"I shone the light around, searching. Under the front corner window, which faces my house and also the street, I found a pair of binoculars. And next to the binoculars, a gun."

"What sort of gun?"

"A revolver with a long barrel. A big metal thing, a kind of cylinder, was fitted to the end of the barrel."

"Silencer," I said.

"Probably. But I didn't know what it was then. I was about to leave when I saw a little cardboard portfolio sticking out from under the bed. I picked it up and opened it. Inside were a couple of letters I had written Larry. Nothing in them really. Harmless

Platonic stuff. But with the letters there was tracing paper, some pencils and a pen. He had been tracing my handwriting.

"There was the rough of a note he must have sent out to God knows how many people. It said, 'I know you did it. I know why you did it and how. When I get the proof, if it's the last thing I ever do, I'm going to send you to the gas chamber.' It was signed 'Barbara.' All of it was in my handwriting. Only an expert could have told the difference."

"God almighty!" I said. "The guy was an absolute nut. He must have had a purpose. What was the point?"

"Well," she said. "We can only guess now. Either he wanted to cause trouble for me—alienate people from me—or he had a plan of some sort."

"It was a marvelous way to get you murdered," I said.

"Or to watch from that room and see who *came* to murder me, expecting to prevent it in time. Maybe he wasn't so sure I did it after all. Maybe he had this little doubt in the back of his mind. So he sends out the notes to every possible suspect and he watches and waits. You'll see how that's logical when I tell you what happened next."

"There was nothing very logical about Vandiver," I said. "I think he was psychotic. Anyway, if he sent out those notes it seems strange that nobody on the receiving end got mad enough to mention it to you, call you a liar or something."

"Oh, but they did! I got a nasty letter and two angry phone calls, one from Stan Spencer, of all people. Of course I denied hotly that I had sent the notes. At the time I thought it must be someone in my own family group who could imitate my writing. I suppose there were others who got notes. But they just hated me in silence."

"It's the silent ones who worry me," I said. "Didn't you inquire if there was anyone else who got one of the notes?"

"No. Because I wasn't on speaking terms with most of my clan. They deserted my little ship the minute it began to sink under the weight of accusation."

"Let's get back to Vandiver and the room at the Tillmans'."

"All right. But the rest of it is stranger still. I took the portfolio with me and left everything else as it was. I went back home and for a while I watched from my window. When Larry didn't return, I got into bed. For a time I lay there trying to put it all together. Then I feel asleep.

"It must have been about two hours later when I heard this feeble kind of scratching or tearing and then a tapping. No, wait a minute! I think before that I was asleep and something awakened me. I have a fuzzy impression, mixed up with a dream, that Grizz was barking. But the first thing I clearly remember was that other sound—the popping one. Soft, like a cork being pulled from a bottle. It's all so confused. After I was fully awake and I kept hearing those sounds, I thought, Why doesn't Grizz bark *now?* But no. Not a peep from him.

"I put on a robe and slippers and tiptoed downstairs. I stood in the center of the living room, listening. I heard the latch turning in the back door. Quiet. Sneaky. I felt like frozen marble. For seconds I couldn't move. Then I dashed for the sofa and hid behind it.

"I heard the back door close softly. Nothing else. So I peered around a corner of the sofa in the darkness. Someone was moving into the room. Creeping."

"Man or woman?"

"I couldn't tell. But it had to be a man, from the size of him and what followed. Anyhow, this is the part that's so unbelievable. I saw someone else moving behind him. And Suddenly he turned and the two of them were fighting. It was horrible. Just little grunts and groans and gasps. Then one of them—I'm certain now it was Larry—ran for the stairs. And bounded up them, with the other right behind, firing that gun that made the weird little sound. I didn't see Larry fall but I heard the thump of his body on the stairs."

"How many shots?" I asked.

"Just one, I think. And then there was a tiny light above. It must have been a flash. It went out almost immediately and I heard him moving around up there—the other one. And I knew he was looking for me. Oh, my God! I didn't breathe! Then he came down finally and drifted out the back door. Gone. I waited there for something like fifteen minutes. Then I went up the stairs and looked.

"It was Larry. And he—he was dead. Later I discovered poor Grizz. I knew the police would never believe my story. So I packed some things and drove to your place. I wanted to tell you everything but I just couldn't. I was afraid you'd be so shocked and suspicious, that you'd never want to see me again."

I told her then. About finding Vandiver myself the day after. And we began to speculate on how it could have happened. We puzzled it half a dozen ways and never could form a completely logical picture of that night.

The best we could do was to guess that Vandiver had come back after Barbara fell asleep. And from the Tillmans' window he had seen someone moving about the house, looking for the best way in. Then Vandiver must have come down with the gun to stop him. And there was a fight in which the killer took the gun away from Vandiver. And since Vandiver was shot twice, but only once in the house, it appeared that he got that first wound in the shoulder outside. He fell and the killer thought him dead. In any case, he recovered and followed the killer into the house. And that was the end of him.

Barbara said, "Do you think the man who killed Larry, trying to get to me, was Frank Imhoff?"

"Or one of his men. There has to be a connection with the bomb murders. But I don't get it. Why would Imhoff want to kill you? And why didn't he do it a long time ago?"

"Because he couldn't find me until recently, when the newspapers gave my address. But more important, now that he's got me here in this house, why hasn't he…"

We sat staring at each other.

"That's a good question," I said. "Why hasn't he? You can

bet he's got a reason for waiting. And a plan. If we sit here long enough we might find out. The hard way. So let's get out of here!"

"Where would we go?"

"Some hotel in New York. Does it matter, as long as you're safe?"

"I'll pack my suitcase," she said.

CHAPTER 16

She went off to the bedroom and I called after her to hurry. While I was waiting I picked up the .22 automatic which she had left on the table. The one she said Imhoff had given her. It was a pretty way to die—death with a pearl handle. I checked the loading slip. It was full. Idly, I wondered if Barbara would know how to work a shell into a chamber.

Then I heard the muted sound of a car on the road. I dropped the gun into my pocket and went to the door. I opened it and peered out. I could see no headlights and now the road was silent and empty. But there had been a car and suddenly I was nervous. I paced the room a couple of times, paused to listen.

"Barbara!" I called. "Will you please hurry?"

She didn't answer and after a moment I went to the bedroom door, knocked and went in.

The light was a small naked bulb dangling from the ceiling. There were twin beds, a scarred bureau and a couple of chairs.

The room was empty.

No suitcase, not a sign that she had been packing.

With a throat gone suddenly dry, I called her name. I new it was only a gesture.

Across the room a longly gust of wind pushed a drawn curtain. I went toward it with the gun in my hand. Behind it, I found the window open. Below, light from the room touched the hard pack of sand with my shadow. I was in a torment **of** mixed emotions. I leaned out. "Barbara!" I called into the night. "Barbara!"

Then I vaulted over the sill.

I didn't hear so much as the whisper of a step behind me. My feet touched, and at the same moment something smashed the back of my head with such force there wasn't time for the fragment of a thought. There was pain. But oblivion swallowed it instantly.

* * * *

I was on my back. I was looking up at the same window. It swam out of the blur into wavering focus. As I watched, another vagrant wind touched the curtain, behind which there was light. My head throbbed and I felt nauseous. I wretched but nothing came. Then all the pain subsided and there was intense clarity.

Looking at the window, I remembered. And had the impression that less than a minute had passed. Somehow, I got to my knees and held my watch to the light. I kept checking and re-checking until I was certain I wasn't being tricked by a distorted brain.

But there wasn't any doubt. Over four hours had gone.

I touched the back of my head. Around the swelling, dried blood caked my hair. I stood, swaying. I leaned against the cottage wall, gulping air. My head throbbed anew. There was nothing in me yet but a grayness of mood.

I climbed back into the room. Unshaded bulb giving the same dismal light. Shabby beds with their cheap chenille spreads, pocked bureau and sagging chairs. Everything as before.

I walked over to the closet, opened it. Dresses on the rack, shoes on the floor. Behind them the polished leather and brassy gleam of an expensive suitcase.

Crossing to the bureau, I saw the note. A folded sheet of ruled paper resting obliquely among jars of cosmetics, as if it had fallen from the mirror frame above. I grabbed it and read:

Darling,

Sorry I had to hit you. But I couldn't let you follow and stop what I am about to do.

It's over, Ross. And don't be very sad. Because I killed them. I made the plan and Larry carried it out. He was just a tool. And when I was through with him, he wouldn't let me go. He might have told it all and I had to silence him.

But there is a limit to endurance. I'm so awfully tired of running. And, too late, I find I am not so strong. There are loathesome images at night and guilt grows like cancer.

I really do love you and perhaps that is the worst of it. Good-bye, Ross.

Barbara

I stumbled to a chair and read the note again. Suicide? Of course. She didn't have to say what was between the lines. I looked at my watch. Four hours and twenty-two minutes. Too late. Much too late to stop her. Even if I wanted to—now.

My God, what a thought! Of course I wanted to stop her. For what? National degradation on the pages of a hundred million newspapers? A sordid trial? Months of waiting in a solitary cell to the last tortured hour before the gas chamber? I could understand how she could find another, faster death more welcome.

I suppose I should have thought her horrible and grotesque. But I didn't. She was merely sad. Immeasurably sad. My feelings had not really jelled. I wanted only to run after her. But where!

I studied the note, especially the handwriting. It seemed to be hers, though her usually neat script wavered over the page in a disorderly scrawl. A kind of hysterical penmanship. Yet the wording was careful enough, almost calmly resigned. A contradiction that puzzled me.

I got out the list of names she had written for me and compared the handwriting. All the characters had the same loops and swirls, the identical touches of individuality. The difference was purely of speed and emotion. It was unmistakably her hand. Still…a nudging doubt wouldn't leave me. The note was vague and it was possible that she meant only to disappear. Again. And finally. But if so, would she leave me such a dangerous confession? Mabye. It would be so convincing. And she could count on me not to expose the note unless her body were found.

I clawed around the room for a clue, opening drawers, her closet, the suitcase, hunting thoroughly and everywhere. One thing struck me immediately. Her pocketbook was missing. And her money. Would a girl about to commit suicide take along her purse and all her cash? Or, much more likely, would she be so despairing, so tortured, that money or possessions would be furthest from her mind, useless in a world she was about to leave?

I went outside and looked for the .25 automatic that had been in my hand when I fell. It was gone. I made a quick search of the grounds, praying not to find her body. I didn't, then I raced to the car and drove insanely to the nearest bar and a phone.

I called the Inn, gave the room number. Dietrich answered sleepily. It was still two hours before he was due to relieve me on the Imhoff watch.

"Christ!" he said irritably. "I toss for a year and then when I do get to sleep—hey, what's up, fella?"

"Trouble," I said. "The worst kind. I found Barbara but—"

"You found Barbara! And that's trouble?"

"Listen, Earl. Please just shut up and listen!"

"My God, man, you sound far out and down. Sorry. I'm listening."

"I gave him the barest details. Enough.

"You're positive she wrote the note herself?" he said.

"Positive."

"That's bad. The part about Vandiver, the whole thing sounds logical, Ross. And if it wasn't true, why would she write it?"

"I still don't believe it."

"Neither do I. What I mean is, I don't want to believe it. But I'm afraid that—oh, hell, forget it. Let's just find her."

"I want to play a hunch," I said.

"I'm with you."

"Then hop over to Imhoff's place and watch."

"For what?"

"See if he comes or goes."

"You still think he might be in this?"

"Yes."

"Long shot," he said. "But worth a try. Okay, I'll get over there and watch. Ten minutes, maybe less. Then what?"

"If he goes in, fine. Just wait for me."

"And if he comes out?"

"There's a gun in my suitcase, .38 police special. Take it and hold him in the car until I get there. I'm gonna sweat him. I'm gonna half kill him, if I have to!"

"Wait a minute, Ross. Don't go off the deep end. I know how you feel, but slide home easy, boy. We can get into a lot of trouble. The legal kind. Even with a character like Imhoff. I think you ought to call the police."

"On what? A hunch?"

"I know but—"

"All right, goddammit," I shouted. "I'll handle him alone!"

"No, you won't. I just want you to use your head. But I'm in. I'll hold that sonofabitch. If he hasn't got company. What about his pals?"

"Hell, they can't sleep with him. Jesus God, just do your best whatever comes. I'm up to here with strain and in a hurry."

"Okay, shove off. Wait! What does he look like?"

I told him.

"How long will you be, Ross?"

"About forty minutes and flying all the way."

I hung up.

It was past 2:00 A.M. Only a few late-nighters pushed for home along the highways. I passed them all, my eyes probing for cops. Once I nearly swallowed a squad car and had to drop behind until he angled off to the right. But in less than forty minutes I was wheeling down tree-shadowed Greenway North, searching out the rented Chevvy and Dietrich.

I found him on a little side street branching off from Greenway. From the mouth of it you could see the Imhoff place obliquely across the street. A good spot. As usual, Dietrich was cool and careful.

I parked behind the Chevvy and walked over. He had the door open and I climbed in beside him.

"No one came or left," he said. "Place is dark. I crept over there and looked. Sedan in the garage. Caddy. Must be his. Bastard's got to be home. Let's go get 'im!"

"How?" I said.

"I like the direct approach," Dietrich answered. "We go up and ring the goddam bell until someone comes. Then we barge in. Behind this." The .38 from my suitcase appeared in his fist. He smiled and the pleasure of action was there on his face. I knew that Imhoff was in for a bad time.

"Let's go!" I said.

We clipped across the street and up to the door. I rang the bell. I really leaned on it. Suddenly there was a flood of light above the door and it opened. Lois Imhoff, pale and sleep-eyed in robe and slippers, stood peering out at us.

"It's Ross Elliot, Mrs. Imhoff," I announced.

"Oh," she said with a little gasp.

"Is your husband in?"

She nodded uncertainly, looking at Dietrich, recognition spreading across her face.

"Earl!" she said. "Earl Dietrich. What are you doing here?"

"It's been a long time, Lois," he said unsmilingly.

"Since the time you flew me to Cuba," she said.

"Where's Imhoff?" I asked.

"Upstairs. He's asleep. What's wrong? You both look so—"

"Something's happened to Barbara," I said.

"To Barb? Oh, God! What?"

"We intend to find out," said Dietrich. "From Imhoff." He pushed past Lois and stepped in. I followed.

"Which way?" I said.

She shook her head. She was obviously frightened and bewildered. "No. Please! I'll go get him."

"Where are the other two?" I asked.

"Not here," she said. "I don't know. But Frank's alone."

"What time did he come in?" said Dietrich.

"Well, he came home early in the evening and went out again. He got back about midnight."

"You just lead the way to his room," I said. "Quietly. That way no one will get hurt."

"Hurt?"

"That's right, Lois," said Dietrich, pulling the gun. "Hurt."

She looked toward the stairs, hesitating.

"Which side are you on?" I said.

"Yeah," said Dietrich. "Which side, Lois?"

She gave us both a long look and then turned without a word and went to the stairs.

They were beautiful stairs, wide and curving, heavily carpeted. Above, we turned left down a hallway. Dietrich followed behind Lois with the gun. We paused at a door and she stepped aside, making a small gesture with her head.

"When we get inside," whispered Dietrich, "where is the light switch?"

She pointed to a position on the wall, right of the door. Dietrich got the picture, slowly turned the knob and went in. I was just behind him. I heard the groping scratch of his fingers. And then light swarmed down from a ceiling fixture.

The covers on the big bed were pulled back, exposing the pink smoothness of satiny sheets. A pillow was mashed. But the bed was empty. Dietrich shot a hard glance at Lois in the doorway. And at that moment I saw Imhoff step out of a closet, his face dark and intent behind the big .45.

"Drop it," said Imhoff quietly, as Earl, catching the movement, swung about.

Dietrich did not drop the gun. He lowered it. Slightly. His face was perfectly bland.

"You pull that trigger, mister," he said, "and they'll fry you like grease in a pan. I'm Lieutenant O'Brien, Homicide." Dietrich let his gun arm fall, as if now it was unimportant. His eyes flicked casually around the room. He seemed really a little bored.

"What do you want with me?" said Imhoff, taking a step forward, canting the .45, holding it less rigidly but not bringing it down. I saw that he wore slacks and a shirt. His feet were bare.

"You're under arrest," said Dietrich. "Harboring a criminal is the charge."

Imhoff took another step, frowning. Worried. "What criminal?"

"Barbara Erickson."

I looked around at Lois, expecting she would give us away at any minute. But she stood mutely with the narrow edge of a smile on her face. She was enjoying it.

Imhoff half lowered the gun. "Oh, now wait a minute, buster," he said. "That's crap you're talking. What proof have you got?"

"Take his gun, Sergeant," commanded Dietrich, turning to me with the face of authority.

"Yes, sir," I said obediently. I marched forward to a position directly in front of him and held out my hand.

"Hold it!" said Imhoff. The gun came up. "You were here this evening. Told me you were a salesman. Real wiseguy." He touched the bruise on his mouth where I had hit him. "Asked my wife and she said, 'That's right, magazine salesman.'"

"Okay," said Dietrich, toying with the .38. "Make it nice and legal, Sergeant. Show him identification."

I peered over my shoulder at him. There was no wink but I caught the message as if it were written in neon across his eyes.

"Yes, sir," I said. But didn't know if I was going to be able to do it with the vast mouth of that .45 looking at my chest.

I reached in my pocket and when I had the wallet upraised in my hand, brought the arm down sharply across Imhoff's wrist. I balled the other hand and chopped his jaw. He did a back bend and the gun fell to the floor.

It wasn't enough. I couldn't hole the angry thing, the fearful thing, inside me. I beat him to the floor. And kept on pounding his face, shouting for him to tell me what happened to Barbara, then not giving him space to answer. Until Dietrich, the .45 in his belt, pulled me off.

"Not here," he said, straddling Imhoff, looking down at the red smear of face. "We'll take him apart and he'll talk. But not here. C'mon! On your feet, slob. On your feet!"

Imhoff got to his knees, stood. He wiped blood from his face with the sleeve of his shirt. He looked sullen, unafraid. He pointed an angry finger at my face.

"You know what you'll get from me?" he hissed. "This!" He slosed two fingers in a circle to form a cipher. "And this!" He spat at me.

Dietrich caught my arm as I brought it back for the punch, shoved Imhoff into a chair. He picked up a pair of shoes by the bed and tossed them. "Put them on!" he ordered.

"What about socks?" said Imhoff.

Dietrich chuckled low in his throat. His jaw worked. "I'll give you socks," he sneered.

Imhoff put the shoes on over bare feet.

We shoved him ahead of us down the stairs. Dietrich gave me the .38 and kept the automatic in his belt.

"Keep your mouth shut," I said to Lois at the door.

She looked suddenly childish and pathetic. I gave her arm a squeeze.

"Maybe it'll be all right," I said.

We went out, marching Imhoff between us. The light narrowed, fading from the walk as Lois slowly closed the door.

CHAPTER 17

We took the Chevvy. Dietrich said that was best because it hadn't been used much and had nearly a full tank of gas. I had put a lot of miles on the Ford and there might not be a gas station open. As soon as Earl mentioned the gas I knew what he was thinking. We didn't have to discuss where to take Imhoff. There was only one place that made any sense. So I took the wheel, we squeezed Imhoff between us and started off.

Nearly all the way to Long Beach we rode in silence. I guess Imhoff expected us to make a loud threatening noise the whole distance. And when we said nothing I could tell it was having a psychological effect on him. He began to fidget. He understood action. But anything passive or subtle, a threat by implication, worried him. In tacit agreement we were setting him up for the kill. Figuratively. Though in truth, I might actually have killed him if that would have saved Barbara.

But there is a time when you have to stop deluding yourself and face the ugliest of facts. Barbara had to be dead. If she was going to commit suicide, she wouldn't wait five or six hours to do it. Suicide is emotional, impulsive. Once you decide upon it absolutely the act follows hard on the thought. Conversely, if the note was phony, engineered by someone else, the next step after it was written was her death to insure secrecy. So Barbara was surely dead. Yet there was one other possibility. The only one which gave me the least hope. Barbara had used the note to camouflage her disappearance. Permanently. In which case Imhoff would probably know where she was.

Whatever he knew, whatever he had done to her, I intended to find out!

I pulled the car into the driveway beside the cottage.

Dietrich said, "This it?"

I told him it was.

"Looks like someone's in there," he said. "Lights on."

"No," I answered. "I didn't turn them out when I left."

Dietrich got out and beckoned Imhoff with a wave of the .45. The front door was unlocked and we went in. Apparently nothing had changed, but I poked around in the bedroom and elsewhere to be certain. I came back and told Imhoff what he must already have known—that Barbara was gone. I showed him the note. Then I placed myself squarely in front of him. I stood looking him in the eye for a full half-minute. The instant he dropped his gaze, I belted him to the floor.

"When I look at you, look back!" I said. "Now get up and stand just where you were. Right here in front of me."

Imhoff got up and stood rigidly before me. His dark, bruised features swam in sweat. Pain and the first of fear were in his eyes. But also hate and rebellion.

"Now," I said. "You stare me in the eye, Imhoff. And you look away just once and see what happens."

His eyes came up to mine and held. There was the feeling that I could see down into his soul. And bring the sewage that was there into the light for inspection.

A half-minute is a long time to look anyone in the eye. A minute is an eternity—if there is the least guilt in you. He didn't make a minute. His eyes began to bulge and shuttle, then to slide from mine.

I hit him. And when Earl stood him before me again, I said, "The next time I'm going to have Dietrich hold you up while I break every bone in your face, bone by bone." My God, I meant it! And he knew that I did.

"We're all alone here, Imhoff," said Dietrich in a voice like doom. "No one's gonna help you. And we're gonna keep hitting and breaking and cutting. Until by morning, Imhoff, you'll be dead."

"All right," I said. "Now look at me! Turn your goddam black evil eyes on me, Imhoff!"

It began again. The sweating and the bulging, the grim staring—iris to iris, pupil to pupil. I saw down deep and the fear was there with the rest of it. And when, after some two lock-eyed minutes, the fear became terror, I said ever so softly, "Tell me, Imhoff."

His jaw worked and his lips moved soundlessly. But I knew he was going to break.

Then a car gunned down the street and braked outside with a squeal of tires. I swung around. Dietrich was striding to the window. There was the quick scuff and clip of feet and the door flew open.

It was Lois Imhoff. She wore a blue cotton dress and she carried one of those shoulder-strap leather pocketbooks. She wore no makeup and an expression of startled concern.

Dietrich sighed mightily. "Lois, for chrissake, why?" he said. "Just when we had it made with this guy."

"I took the Cadillac and followed," she said. "I was worried. I thought maybe you might…" She trailed off and stood gazing anxiously at Imhoff, who sank to the edge of a chair. He looked at her, but not with any show of relief, or anything at all. Just a look.

"Don't think it's over, Imhoff," I said. "We're just beginning."

"Isn't Barbara here," said Lois to no one in particular. And when she didn't get an answer: "Maybe he doesn't really know after all. Do you, Frank?"

Imhoff stared at her silently, kneading his fingers. She crossed to him, studied his battered face, reached out a hand to touch him, withdrew it. She turned to us.

"I want to find Barbara as much as you do," she said. "But this brutality… I was afraid you might kill him."

"Oh, shut up!" said Imhoff suddenly, and with great disgust.

"We might kill 'im," said Dietrich, nodding. "We might kill 'im at that. If he doesn't talk."

"After all," said Lois, hurrying on, pleading, "he's my husband. And though we've had our differences, I do have *some* feeling for him. Even some love." She turned to him. "Yes, I do, Frank, I do." She began to cry. "Please let him alone. For just a minute while I try and talk to him."

"Shut up!" said Imhoff again. "You righteous bitch!"

"Why, Frank!" she gasped.

"Love," he sneered. *"Please don't hurt Frank,"* he mimicked. *"Leave my Frank alone.* You slut! He looked at me. "You wanna know what happened to your Barbara? Well, don't ask me. I know from nothing. Ask her." He pointed at Lois. "Ask her, she knows."

"Liar!" said Dietrich. "Shut your mouth, Imhoff."

"No, wait a minute," I said. "Let's hear what he has to say."

"Why, Frank," Lois said. "I come down here practically begging for your life, and you turn on me."

"Begging for my life," Imhoff groaned. "You'd let them beat me to death and stand there cheering. But you're afraid they might hear something before I died. Ask her how she found this place."

"I told you, Frank. I followed behind in the Cadillac."

"You did, huh? And had time to get dressed from the ground floor? We flew outta there in—what? Maybe thirty seconds, a minute. And you were in a nightgown. Don't make me laugh!"

"Hey, that's right," said Dietrich.

"What about it, Lois?" I snapped.

"So I've been here before," said Lois, undisturbed. "I have ways of finding out things, too. I followed Frank the other day."

"That right?" said Imhoff. "In whose car? We have just one, you know."

"That's my business," she answered, moving away from his chair.

"No," I said. "It's not. It's ours now."

"I'll tell you guys the truth," said Imhoff. "I've been protecting the bitch. Because until now, I didn't know the score. She gave me a snow job and I thought Barbara was still here, that she was okay."

"This guy stinks," said Dietrich. "He's hiding behind a woman."

"Maybe," I said. "We'll see. Go on, Imhoff."

"I was here tonight—earlier. Barbara was fine. We talked and I left. I've got boys who'll vouch for me, that she was okay. When I got home, Lois was gone. She came in about three hours later, around midnight. She thought I was asleep, but I heard her on the stairs. I got up and put on a robe. I crossed the hall to her bedroom and walked in. She was sitting on the edge of the bed, counting some dough. A bunch of it. Hundred dollar bills.

"I asked her where she got it, and she said it was none of my business. There was a wallet on the bed, a fancy one with little jewels. I picked it up and looked at the papers in it. Whose wallet? Barbara's!"

"Liar!" cried Lois from across the room.

"Barbara's!" shouted Imhoff. "Said she borrowed a car, followed us out here and waited till we were gone. Then she went in and got cozy with Barbara, she told me. And Barbara gave her the money to keep because it was dangerous to have so much around, out here all alone. Well, it made just enough sense that I believed her until I could check in the morning. But we had a fight about it. Then I went to bed.

You guys came with the bad news and that's it. That's all I know. You don't believe me, take a look in that bag and see if she's got the wallet with her."

"That's ridiculous!" said Lois, opening the bag and reaching in. "Here. I'll show you."

She showed us the barrel end of a small caliber automatic.

"I'm a very good shot," she said.

Imhoff was the only one who didn't believe her, or didn't care. He got up and took a step toward her. "That looks like the .25 I gave Barbara," he said.

"And if you want a small, very hard part of it back, darling," said Lois, "just come and get it."

Imhoff got the point. He didn't try it.

"Lois," I said. "Is she—is she dead?"

"Sorry, sweetie," said Lois. And I heard the words distantly, as if echoed in a tunnel. "Sorry, but it was worth a million to me and I adore money. You see, Barbara left me everything. We were very close."

My lips moved numbly, trying to form the word. "How?" I said.

"She went for a swim," Lois said coolly. "And she drowned."

I thought, Well, she's only a woman, it's a small gun and there are three of us. I turned to Dietrich and I said just that. "There are three of us, Earl. And she won't get us all."

Lois looked at Dietrich and smiled. "How many, Earl?" she said. "How many are there really?"

"Two!" pronounced Dietrich. The .45 was in his hand and he had stepped quickly to her side.

"Shoot them," she said. "It's the only way now."

Dietrich looked at the .45, said, "Not with this. Did you bring the other one?"

"With the silencer? In the car I'll get it." She went out.

"She's such a help," said Dietrich, smiling. But I could see he was nervous. He hadn't planned on killing so many.

In a minute the door opened and Lois stepped in. She didn't have a weapon. And she wasn't alone. The uniformed officer had the weapon—a riot gun which he held to the back of Deitrich's head. The plainclothes man had the .38 with the silencer. He showed it to Dietrich, said, "This what you're looking for, buddy?"

That was when he took the .45 from Detrich and cuffed him and Lois together. Then we all went out to the squad car.

Barbara Erickson was in the back seat, and when she saw us coming, she got out quickly. She passed Dietrich and Lois on the way to me, and she paused, blocked their path. Then she slapped them each once across the face, a hard vicious blow.

She ran to me then. And I held her and she stopped my questions with a finger on my lips. Together we watched them go, Imhoff up front with the uniformed driver, the two prisoners and the plainclothes man in back.

"We have to follow soon, you know," she said. "Down to the station. But I can show you. I was there just awhile ago."

We took the Chevvy, the one I had rented. On the way she told me.

There had been a young couple nestling on a lonely stretch of beach, just kids, really. And they had seen her being dragged to the water by the big blond man in bathing trunks and the woman with the odd-looking gun. And they were frightened for their own lives and terribly silent. But they whispered and the girl crawled away to call the police while the young man waited until the couple with the gun had gone. Then he ran for the surf.

He would have been too late anyway. But Barbara, submerged beneath Dietrich's shoving feet and powerful hands, had a dying inspiration. She stopped struggling. She went limp and stayed limp. And when he let go, she made herself sink. Then, almost unconscious, she swam weakly off underwater and surfaced in the dark, floating a little, fading fast. But the young man found her as she was washing ashore unconscious. And the police came as he was working over her with his small knowledge of artificial respiration. The ambulance took her to a hospital in time. But it was hours before she fully recovered and told a coherent story. And by then I was gone from beneath the window.

So she waited with the police behind the cottage, guessing that I had gone for Dietrich and he would play dumb and return with me.

Of course Dietrich and Lois were secret lovers. He met her every time he flew to New York. And of course Dietrich made the bomb and planted the package in the car. And Lois supplied the anniversary card—a forgotten one found in a desk and written by Barbara the year before. The motive was at first the much greater sum of money Lois expected Harvey Erickson to leave her. And later Barbara's better than a million which she left Lois "because, of the whole family, she was the only one who still *appeared* to give me loyalty and love."

And of course Dietrich killed Vandiver, who got between him and Barbara. And grabbed her in the cottage bedroom. And lay in waiting to club me outside, while Lois held Barbara silent. And then forced her to write the note, holding a gun to my head and threatening to finish me.

I drove slowly, listening in a dream happiness to a nightmare. And when she had said it all, I pulled off the road and we kissed until our lips were bruised.

But then she murmured, "Hurry, darling, and let's be done with it at the station. And after, oh, God, I don't ever want to look at them again."

It was in that dark hour before dawn, and the police station, with its green light suspended above the entrance, had a look of hushed solemnity and sleeping isolation. As if justice slumbered too, delaying punishment for a harsher time of wakefulness and dispatch.

It was as we climbed the steps that I reached in my pocket and handed her the note—the false one with its tone of suicide between every line.

"Give it to them for evidence," I said. "It was shudderingly convincing."

"They composed it long ago," she said. "With such loving care."

"And forgot one thing," I added. "If I know anything about the law, they wouldn't have gotten a penny."

"I don't understand. Why?"

"Because according to the note, you killed your father. And if the note was believed, then as his killer you had no legal right to his inheritance. And if you had no legal right to it, you couldn't leave it to anyone else. Result—the money would have gone to the nearest blood relative of your father. And that wasn't Lois."

"Oh, I hate them," she said. "I hate them! But they're very

sad, don't you think?"

"Yes," I said. "Very."

Then I took her hand. And together we entered the building.

ABOUT THE AUTHOR

Robert Colby says: "I began writing while in the South Pacific, invading Jap-held islands with the Army Infantry during World War II. After the war I wrote hit-or-miss for a year or two, then began to study, take private lessons, and attend creative writing courses. I wrote on-and-off for about seven years before I sold my first story to a magazine that promptly collapsed just after sending me a check!

"I then began to write novels and made my first sale, a novel, to Ace Books. Meanwhile, I held down a radio and TV announcer's job at various stations around the country—NBC in New York, CBS in Hollywood, KOA in Denver, WBEN in Buffalo, and WAVE in Louisville, to name a few. Most of the time I would announce half the night and write all the next day. For the past four years I have been writing full time. My wife and I live in a house on the banks of New River in Fort Lauderdale, Florida, one room of which has been converted into an office."

Made in the USA
Middletown, DE
26 October 2021